WE CALLED HIM BOSS

BUD GARDNER

outskirts
press

Outskirts Press, Inc.
http://www.outskirtspress.com

Paperback ISBN: 978-1-9772-4352-2

PRINTED IN THE UNITED STATES OF AMERICA

Table of Contents

PREFACE

In 1973 I was a Correctional Officer in the Maximum Security Facility of the Adult Correctional Institution of the Department of Social and Rehabilitative Services in the State of Rhode Island, later becoming the Rhode Island Department of Corrections. The Maximum Security Facility was a large gray stone, castle like, structure built in 1878.

One day I was assigned to take a detail of inmates into the attic of the institution to empty it of everything that had been placed there over the last almost 100 years. There were boxes of old books, files, broken chairs and benches, all covered with several inches of dirt, dust mixed with several inches of pigeon dropping. In the far corner of the attic was a desk, with fancy turned legs, and carved front. It was piled with collapsing boxes of books and papers, all covered with a substantial layer of droppings. As the inmates were clearing the boxes off the desktop. I opened the center draw. Inside there were several old ink pens along with some notes on scraps of paper. The writing was old script written by a fine hand. Opening the right side draw, I found an old set of handcuffs and a file folder containing hand written letters to Warden Nelson Viall. The left drawers had written material and a variety of other folders. I soon came to the conclusion that this was the desk that belonged to Nelson Viall, the Warden of the Rhode Island State Prison built almost 100 years earlier. As the inmates continued to empty the attic of the "trash", I continued to look through the files and papers, placing them into a box. I set the box aside and took a broom and swept the desk top of the debris. The beauty of the old desk became more evident. In the center of the desk top was a walnut diamond shape inlay. The desk seemed to be made of chestnut. The front was false draws matching the working draws on the back of the desk, each ornately carved. I thought, this is my desk, I want this. I called the officer in the carpenter shop and told him I had found an old desk I was sending over, and wanted it cleaned up but not re-finished to put on my post in the segregation unit. He said fine send it over. At that time the segregation unit was my regular post assignment five days a week. I set the box of papers that was inside the desk aside along with a ledger that was in the bottom left draw aside. At the end of the day I took the box of papers and the ledger to my car. The ledger book turned out to be the account book for the "Debtor's Prison" containing the prisoner's name, date of commitment and what he owed to whom. On my day off I took the box to the Rhode Island Historical Society. They were thrilled to receive the items.

The desk was brought from the carpenter, shop to the segregation unit. I bought the officer lunch. Called the Deputy Warden and told him that I had found "A Desk" in the attic and wanted to use it on my post. "OK sure that's fine. He told me." Done Deal! That desk followed me throughout my career at the Department of Corrections. From Maximum, to the Training Academy, to Chief of Security, and to my office as Deputy Warden, Warden and Assistant Director. That was my desk. I fully intended to take it with me when I retired, but chickened out. When I retired I left it behind. The last thing I needed was to be charged with stealing State Property, upon retiring. A retirement party was thrown for me a few weeks after my retirement. The Department Director A. T. Wall stood to give a speech. As he spoke a large item was rolled out covered by a sheet. I jokingly asked if that was my coffin. When the sheet was removed it was "My Desk." The Director had bought it from the State for a dollar, had a small plaque made for it thanking me for over 30 years of service to the Department. The desk, now truly mine, is in my home office.

Over the years, I looked into the life of Warden

Nelson Viall. I felt that I should know more about him and his life, seeing we both have sat behind the same desk.

In 1979, while a Lieutenant, I was in charge of the Training Academy of the Department of Corrections. On a shelf, covered in dust I found a book written by Dr. Henry A. Jones, The Dark Days of Social Welfare at the State Institutions at Howard, Rhode Island. The book was about the "Early Days" of the State Institutions, which included the State Prison and Providence County Jail along with the Poor Farm and Mental Institutions. As I looked through the pages, he described how he was a young doctor when he went to work at the state prison as its first full time physician. His book spoke about a number of events in the prison at the time and his interaction with the Warden, Nelson Viall. I was hooked. These two individuals were total opposites in their approach towards inmates and how they should be treated. Warden Viall was a hard liner, veteran of two wars. Commanding men in combat, an Ex-Police Chief, and longtime Prison Warden. A real no nonsense guy, large and in charge. While the good Doctor Jones was a true reformer, young and looking to improve the lot of the poor and underdog. Both coming together within the stone walls of the State Prison, each with their own mission.

When I retired in 2001, I decided to try and write a book about these two dedicated professionals. Not a historical novel, but a fictional story, based on their differences and possible interactions on events that took place and may have taken place behind the walls. The lesser characters, and conversations between the Doctor and the Warden, are from the imagination of the author, or from the whispers in my ear from the General as I sat at his desk. Keeping in mind the saying "What happens in prison stays in prison". Other things kept getting in the way of writing for nineteen years. But in 2020 with a pandemic, and having to stay at home I have found the time.

WARDEN'S DESK

FOREWORD

Late in the nineteenth century the lives of two men crossed in the confines of a gray stone castle, the Rhode Island State Prison. Two men who were of opposite mind sets. One whose life was dedicated to the service of his State and Nation, and the protection of society. The other a reformer who dedicated his life to changing society and enlightening it to become a more compassionate and caring society.

In this point in time, less than thirty years had passed since the Great War between the states had ended. The hardships of the embattled troops was still fresh in the minds of those who had sacrificed so much to maintain the nation and its social structure. People with mental illness, low intelligence, physical defects and the criminal element, were removed from society and locked away. They were not only separated from society physically but also socially. They were out of sight and out of mind. The conditions by which they were kept was of no concern to the average citizen. These "lesser" members of humanity were placed in institutions to be "cared for". Thus keeping society safe from their criminal ways and or their polluting respectable society. The plight of those institutionalized and the conditions under which they lived was not confined to just this country. The conditions, and the treatment of those incarcerated in these institutions were the thinking of mainstream society throughout the U.S. and Europe.

Nelson Viall was born November 27 1827 in Plainfield, Connecticut. Nelson did not have an easy life. He had to depend on himself for food, shelter and other resources. His hard life helped him become a fit and strong young man, giving him determination to succeed in whatever he undertook, the grandson of a Colonel in the War of 1812. When the war with Mexico broke out in 1847 he enlisted as a private, then corporal, then sergeant in Company A, Ninth Infantry U.S. Volunteers. During the war he participated in the battles of Conteras, Cherubusco, and aided in the conquering of the capital of Mexico. Upon returning to Providence R.I. he was employed as a moulder. With the onset of the Civil War, Nelson enlisted as a Lieutenant in the 1st R.I. Militia, raised and commanded by Colonel Ambrose Burnside. When the unit mustered out he received a commission as a Captain and commanded Company D of the 2nd R.I. Volunteer Infantry. Distinguishing himself at the 1st Battle of Bull Run in July of 1861, Viall was promoted to Major. A confident and strong combat leader. In December of 1862, Lt. Colonel Viall assumed command of the regiment. Following the Battle of Fredericksburg he was promoted to full Colonel. Over his dissatisfaction and trouble arising from the appointment of the chaplain to the rank of major, he resigned in January of 1863. But, after a short period of inaction, He was commissioned as Lt. Colonel of an African American unit, 14th R.I. Colored Heavy Artillery, designated as the 11th U.S. Colored Heavy Artillery. The unit served garrison at New Orleans in defense of the city and surrounding area. Soon after the end of the war he received a colonel's commission from Washington, together with the promotion to the rank of Brigadier General by brevet.

Upon his return to Rhode Island, Nelson was named Chief of Police in Providence. Then in 1867 Nelson was named Warden of the RI State Prison. He served as Warden of the State Prison/County Jail until his death on May 1, 1903.

Dr. Henry A. Jones was born in England in 1870. Doctor Jones moved to the United States becoming a citizen on April 7, 1900. Seven years earlier he was appointed by Dr. George Keene, Medical Superintendent of the State Institutions at Howard, to be Physician for the State Prison and Providence County Jail. The Institutions consisted of the State Almshouse, Asylum for the Insane, House of Correction for Men and Women (State Farm), the State Prison, Providence County Jail and the Sockanosset School for Boys and the Oaklawn School for girls.

Dr. Jones was a young Physician, Idealistic and eager to serve humanity and better the lot of the poor and downtrodden of society. Throughout the nineteenth century and before, the treatment of the poor, orphans, mentally ill, and the imprisoned was deplorable. The Author, Charles Dickens, a social reformer of the time, described the plight of the outcasts of society in his novels, A Christmas Carol, and Oliver Twist. Dr. Jones viewed his appointment as Doctor for the State Prison as an opportunity to improve the lives of the prisoners as well as attending to their medical needs. All of the conditions that existed in the State Institutions were not entirely the fault of the state government. They were due, in a great measure, to the spirit of the times and the limited education of the day toward public welfare. The Civil War was still fresh in the mind of the public. The veterans and their families were not in the mood for flowers and luxurious things of life. They had seen wartime suffering in the defense of their nation. They witnessed ill-fed in rags, ill and wounded dying on fields of battle, and considered the poor, the afflicted, and the prisoner extremely fortunate to have a dry, warm bed and sufficient food.

The Rhode Island State Prison moved from its original location in Providence to a new facility in Howard section of Cranston in 1878. The old prison was built in 1838. Warden Viall was appointed Warden of the old prison in June of 1867. Upon the opening of the Prison in Howard, Warden Viall marched, without incident, the inmate population from Providence to the new facility. By April of 1893, when Dr. Jones was assigned as physician, Warden Viall had been the Prison Warden for 26 years. The "BOSS", he was large and in charge. Within the walls he was in command and his word was law. He was known by the leaders of the state government and strong and capable administrator.

The coming together of these two individuals would prove to be a test of wills and period of learning and compromise compelling both men to work towards bringing the State Prison and Providence County Jail into the twentieth century.

PROVIDENCE POLICE 1800's

*STATE PRISON/PROVIDENCE
COUNTY JAIL 1900'S*

Dedicated to those men and women who work the
toughest beat in the state.

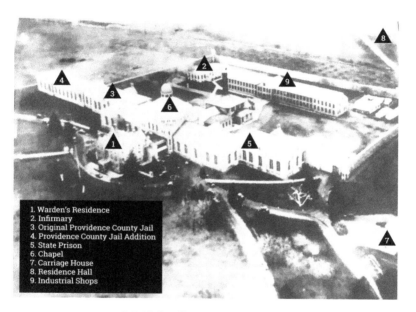

1. Warden's Residence
2. Infirmary
3. Original Providence County Jail
4. Providence County Jail Addition
5. State Prison
6. Chapel
7. Carriage House
8. Residence Hall
9. Industrial Shops

PRISON/JAIL GROUNDS

CHAPTER 1
THE END

As I walked up the walkway of the Warden's residence on this cool Thursday April 30, 1903 morning, I was hoping against hope to find some improvement in the Boss's condition. I have watched his health decline in recent weeks. He has become more congested and his heart is being affected. His color has become a yellowish gray. I am extremely concerned. The General has had quite a life, fighting two wars and the stress of running a state prison for over 35 years. He has had quite a life and it has taken its toll on his body.

I knocked on the large oak door of the gray stone residence that stood in front of the State Prison. In a few minutes the door swung open, standing in front of me was a thirty something, auburn haired, women in a day dress her hair styled in a bun in the back of her head.

"Good morning, Maureen, and how are you this

fine day."

"Oh, fine, fine, doctor, and yourself?" She greeted in a slight Irish brogue.

I replied, "I'm well, how is the boss doing this morning?"

"Oh, doctor the General is not doing well at all. He seems to be getting weaker each day. This morning, when I arrived, I found him at his desk lying face down. I thought he was dead. Saints preserve us, he scarred the devil out of me he did. He must have been there all night. I touched him on his shoulder and he opened one eye and looked at me, and said. "Do you need something, Maureen? Why are you still here?" "I told the General it was morning, and he needed to go straight to his bed. I called for the Captain to send a guard to help me with him. The guard helped him into his night shirt and we put him to his bed."

"Has the General been eating?" I asked the housekeeper.

"Not as you would call a proper meal, doctor. I have gotten him to take some small portions of potato and vegetables and a bit of chicken. However, not but three days put together, would make a true meal for a man his size."

I thought, the General had found a gem of a housekeeper. Maureen Flynn, was the widow of one of the boss's prison guards, Richard, who was passed away three years ago, leaving her with two young children. The General has had several housekeepers since his wife Mary passed away in "94", a little less than a year after my being hired as the prison physician. Maureen is a hard worker who keeps a fine house and has cared for the Warden well since she has been in his employ. I have often thought to myself, what a strong women she is. She is most respectful towards the General, especially in the presents of others, but her Irish roots and red hair does not tolerate the idea of any disrespect or taking advantage of her position by her employer.

"I was putting the pot on for some tea for the General and myself. Would you like a spot of tea, doctor?"

"That would be wonderful, Maureen it is a damp April morning and I am a little chilled from my walk over."

Maureen told me to go ahead to the Warden's bedroom and that she would be up with the tea in a few minutes. Grabbing my small black medical bag, I climbed the stairs to the Boss's bedroom on the second floor. I knocked lightly on the door.

"Come in Maureen," I heard called out in raspy voice. "Oh, sorry Doctor Jones, I thought it was Maureen." The room was a little dark with the drapes drawn. I could see him in his bed, lying half sitting up, in his light green night shirt. "Thank you for stopping by to check up on me, doctor." He said between several raspy coughs. "If I knew that you were coming so early in the morning, I would be up and dressed." It was just before eleven o'clock, five hours after the General's normal waking. I would not embarrass him by revealing the true time.

"I was speaking with Maureen and she was telling me she found you this morning at your desk. Gave her quite a scare you did."

He smiled and gave a phlegm laced laugh. "Poor women, she thought I was dead. I must have fallen asleep doing some paper work last night." There was a soft, almost hesitant knock at the bedroom door. I rose and opened it. Maureen was there with a pot of tea and two Chinese porcelain tea cups. She set the tray down on the side table. "Let me open these curtains and let some light in." The room lit up with the early spring sun. I could now better see my patient. Maureen was right. He did appear much worse than when I had seen the General the morning before.

"Won't you join us for tea, Maureen?" The Warden asked.

"No, No, thank you Sir, I'll be to my work. I have my tea in the kitchen. You gentlemen visit. Doctor, if you could stop and see me before you leave. I'd like to ask you medical opinion on my daughter."

"Sure, I will see you on my way out," I replied as she left closing the door. "Fine women you have there, Warden."

"She is that." the General replied.

I helped the Warden with his tea, holding it as not to spill the hot liquid on him or the bedding. He sipped the warm tea, it seemed to clear his throat of the phlegm, and brighten his gaze. "AR, Nothing like a bit of tea when you are ailing doctor." A fine tradition you English have, too bad we had to throw so much of it in the ocean." The first spark in the General's eye I've seen in a while. He does enjoy needling me over the troubles our countries have had over history, even though I became a citizen of these United States three years ago.

"Now, let me check you out, General." I opened my bag and took out my stethoscope, placing it to his broad chest, "Hold your breath, alright breath." He expelled his breath in a series of coughs. "Now, sit up a little. I want to listen to your lungs." I placed the stethoscope to his back. "Take a deep breath, again, again." Checking both lungs. He went into a fit of coughing, taking several minutes to catch his breath. The General's heart was labored, and both lungs were full. I took his temperature, even with just having a sip of tea it was normal. I took a hold of his wrist and his pulse appeared weak. Throwing back the sheets and blanket, I examined his feet. The ankles were swollen, I noticed a large scar on his right foot. "What happened here?" The General told me that it was an old wound from the Mexican War.

"I was in the battle of Chepultepec, I was wounded ascending one of the storming ladders when that happened. I was a Corporal at that time. It never did heal completely. It does give me some problems every now and then." I commented that I hadn't known that he was wounded in that war also. "I'm a very fortunate man, Doctor. "I have an overworked Guardian Angel." He chuckled.

"Hum, Nelson," I rarely called him by his first name as he rarely called me Henry. Even though over the last ten years we have become close colleagues within the prison. Out of respect for each other and especially with others present we seldom used first names. "You are not doing too well. You really need to be put into the hospital. I will make the arraignments and have your Deputy get you transported there. You need to be placed in an oxygen tent to help you breath. You are taxing your heart and could die without constant oxygen."

"I know what you are saying, Henry, but I am not going to the hospital. People go into the hospital to die. You're a good doctor, Henry, I trust you. I've seen your work, especially during the typhoid problem here, the men you treated got better, while the ones sent to the hospital many didn't make it." I knew my efforts to convince him to go into the hospital was a waste of time, but I needed to impress upon him the importance that he needs to go. "Warden, if you stay here at home, you will die here at home."

He looked into my eyes and said, "Doctor, I am staying home. Here I have work to do. Many times I have looked upon the angel if deaths, I long ago stopped fearing him."

"But, Warden!" I interrupted.

His voice became clear and resolute. "Doctor! I

am not going to the hospital. That's my decision. And, that is the final decision. Why? Because I'm the fucking Boss! And that is it."

I sat back down and took his hand. Shaking hands, I told him I would do my best for him and that I would see him every day to check up on him. He said, "I know you will Henry, and I know you will do all that you can for me. If I shouldn't come back from this, I don't want you blaming yourself, nor will anyone think the less of you or that you provide poor care to me." I told him I would see him tomorrow morning and wished him a peaceful night. I put the tea cups on the tray and took the tray and my bag, leaving the General to rest.

I entered the kitchen to find Maureen seated at the table with an empty cup. She stood to greet me. I told her to please sit, and took a seat next to her. "How is the General, doctor?"

"Not well, not well at all Maureen. I recommended he go to the hospital for oxygen treatment, but he would not hear of it. He absolutely refuses to go. Maureen, I need your help with him. I have a treatment that I would like you to apply to the General's chest." I reached into my bag and took out a jar containing Vicks, Croup and Pneumonia Salve that would open up his clogged lungs, also reduce his cough, and handed it to her. "This needs to be applied three times a day, once in the morning before breakfast, again at noon and lastly at night at bed time. If you could be so kind as to assist me with this. Also Maureen, the

General shouldn't be alone in the house. Would you be able to stay over to keep a check on him? I will return early in the morning to check on how he is doing."

"Oh, doctor I would be glad to do the treatments, but, I would not be able to stay through the night. What would people be thinking of me, a widow women and the General a widower and, my employer all night together in this grand house. Then there's my children I have to tend to at my home. I will forgo my day off to work here until his health return, please God, or I am not needed, Heaven forbid."

"I understand, Maureen. I will have the Deputy Assign one of his most dependable guards to stay in the house and check on him throughout the night."

"You know doctor, I would if I could, but the children you know. They only have me. It is not so much the wagging tongues of the old crones, but the children. He is a wonderful man and employer. When Richard, my grand and loving husband passed away, the General took me on so I was able to care for the children and keep my family together. Without him, my children would be taken from me, with not penny of income coming to the house."

I took her hand and said I understood and told her she is a good women and friend to the Warden. I stood and took my leave, saying I would see her tomorrow. I went into the prison and asked Deputy Slocum to provide a good man to watch over the Warden through the night until the housekeeper returned. He was most concerned about the Warden and his health and offered to stay himself if need be. I thanked him and left for home the sun was already setting and I still had some reports to write on other patients.

I arrived at the residence hall and walked into the parlor. There were several other residents seated around the room talking. I greeted them together. "Good afternoon gentlemen." They asked me to join them. Before doing so I walked to the liquor cabinet and poured myself a glass of brandy. Taking a sip, I went over and sat down with the group. They mentioned that I looked as if I had had a bad day. "It's the Warden, he is very ill and is refusing to go to the hospital."

"You know what he is like, Henry. He can be a stubborn man at times." I raised my eyes towards Heaven saying to myself, sometimes. The conversation moved on and so did the time. After finishing my drink I excused myself telling them that I still had some work to catch up on and, wished them a goodnight. Reaching the top of the stairs, I walked down the hall to my apartment. I removed my jacket and tie, and after kicking off my shoes I took a seat at the desk. I rolled the top up and opened one of the patient files to study the case. This inmate was doing time for murder. I had not seen Martin Dalton since 1894 when he moved from the jail wing to the prison wing. He had a persistent cough and I was worried he may be suffering from tuberculosis. If so I needed to isolate him in the infirmary.

After I finished my work. I sat on the couch and put my feet up. My mind kept wondering back to my years as the Prison Physician. It's hard to believe that it has been ten years since I stepped off the train at the Howard Depot to start my assignment at the prison. It has been quite a journey so far. I closed my eyes and pictured that snowy morning in 1893..........

CHAPTER 2
OPPORTUNITY KNOCKS

My interview went well with the Board of Charities and Corrections. Following my interview, I was sent by Chairman Coggeshall, to meet with Dr. George Keene. Doctor Keene is the Deputy Superintendent for the Asylum for the Insane. I had heard of his efforts in improving the conditions for those sent to the State Institutions, at Howard in Cranston. Dr. Keene had developed a reputation of being a forward thinking physician in the area of public health. He had won a number of battles with the Legislature on funding for improvements at the Alms House and the Institution for the Insane. Other states were progressing to a higher order in the treatment of the insane, feeble-minded, the poor and prisoners. While Rhode Island was backwards in its thinking and treatment of those who occupied the lowest rung of the social ladder. All of the blame for the treatment of the occupants of the State Facilities was not entirely the legislature's fault. In some measure it is due to the thinking of the public of our time, and the limited education of our day toward public welfare. The public considers the poor, the afflicted and the prisoner extremely fortunate to have a dry, warm bed and sufficient food. The general citizens of society thinks it to be a weakness in the individual in authority at the institutions to give way to any thought of "coddling" those whose support comes from their hard earned tax dollars.

I stood in front of a large, highly polished, oak door. A brass name plate to its right read, Office of the Deputy Superintendent. I smiled to myself and thought how frugal. By not putting the name of the good doctor on the name plate, the state would save the cost of changing the brass plaque every time the occupant of the office would change. I took a deep breath and knocked.

"Come in." A voice called out from within. I turned the heavy brass door knob, and entered. Sitting behind a large mahogany desk was a well-dressed man of medium build, appearing much younger than I had expected. A name plate standing at the front of the desk read "Dr. George F. Keene". Seated in a leather easy chair, to his right, was another gentleman. "Come in, come in, welcome". Standing, he came around his desk to greet me, taking my hand with a firm hand shake. "You must be Dr. Jones. I'm George Keene, it's so nice to meet you. Let me introduce you to my dear friend and colleague

Dr. McCaw." He stood and also reached for my hand to greet me. "Dr. McCaw is an Assistant Physician here at the institution. He assists us daily from eight o'clock until noon. Bill has his practice in Providence and is kind enough to help us here, where ever he is needed. Please take a seat." The doctor gestured to another matching leather chair to the left of his desk. "Well Henry, May I call you Henry? It can get confusing with all the doctor titles flying around." Both the men started laughing and I joined in. "Feel free to call me George. May I call you Henry?"

"Of course, please, Henry is fine." I took my seat, feeling much more relaxed than I had expected in the company of a man whom I had admired for what he has accomplished with the poor souls under his care. "Doctor, uh, George, it is such an honor to meet you. I have heard of your work at the institutions, and your efforts to improve treatment and conditions here. Truthfully, one of the reasons I applied for the Physician's position at the State Institutions, is to offer, what skills I may have, to bring better care and comfort to the souls living here."

"Well, thank you Henry, that's very kind of you. I have been informed, unofficially of course, by the Chairman of the Board that the Board is approving your being engaged in a full time position here at the Institutions. If you accept the position, the Board is prepared to offer you a salary of $750.00 per year, also, room and board here on the grounds. I want to be honest with you, at this time our greatest need is for a full time Physician at the Providence Jail and State Prison. Which would be your primary assignment. Of course, if need be, you would be on call at any of the facilities on the grounds. You would be fairly compensated for any extra duties. I do not need your decision at this time but, I wanted to let you know early to give you an opportunity to think about your decision. I believe, it could be a good opportunity for a young physician, such as yourself, to gain a great deal of experience quickly."

"Thank you, George. I was not expecting to find out the board's decision today. The offer does sound exciting and challenging, and it is a great opportunity for me. I'm sure you know that I am not yet a citizen of your great country."

"That does not pose a problem, Henry, you are recognizes and board certified by the State. And, should you wish to become a citizen I would be happy to sponsor your application."

"Thank you, Doctor. I believe I will take you up on the offer in the future." At this point my head is spinning on how rapidly things are moving. Becoming the full time physician for the Jail and Prison at my age is the chance of a lifetime. Working with a man with the reputation of Doctor Keene, and moving the cause of better treatment of society's poor and forgotten forward will give me great joy.

"Henry, I would like you and Bill to spend some time together talking about working in the prison. He has been working part time there for a couple of years now. It can be a most difficult assignment caring for the criminal element of our state. Not to mention working closely with the principal administrator, Warden Viall. He can be difficult at times. He is a fair man but strict in his operation of the institution. Bill has made a number of changes in medical procedures recently and has developed a good working relationship with the General. I have asked Bill to show you around, and take you over to the Physician's living quarters. I hope seeing where you would be living, and meeting some of the other doctors in residence here, will help you in deciding to accept the position. You should be receiving a letter from the Board of Charities and Corrections in the next couple of days with the offer I have outlined to you. Once you receive the letter come back and see me. Hopefully, you will accept the position. I look forward to working with you."

I could have given him my enthusiastic acceptance of the position right then and there. I was truly excited to become part of the work being done in public health within the State of Rhode Island. Doctor McCaw and I bid our good byes to Doctor Keene and headed out of the Administration Building walking west along the main road going through the institutions. The sun was strong, but a cold March breeze blew at the openings of our overcoats. We turned left and walked down a slight incline. The rear of the castle like prison stood below us. Our vantage point gave us a view into the prison yard. Bill pointed out the building in the right hand corner of the yard was the infirmary, with cement finished walls painted white. The large rectangular stone building, in the center of the yard, contained the prison workshops. At each corner of the wall, surrounding the prison, standing on top of the wall were guard posts. To the left of the workshops was a small stone building. I was told that this building was where soap was made from lard and lie rendered from the farm animals. Enough soap to supply all the facilities. We turned left and went up a walkway leading to a large brick building. "Here we are Henry, this is the Physician's residences." We entered the front door walking into an open foyer. In front of us was a table, behind the table was a tall grandfather clock. To the right and left were stair cases leading to the second floor. "Why don't we go into the parlor and get to know one another." Bill took the lead and turned left and walked a short distance into a large paneled room. Several large chairs were scattered about arraigned so the occupants could converse in groups of two or three. A large couch was the center point of the seating. Each chair had an end table, the couch was furnished with an end table at each arm. Several display cases were spread along the walls, and a small china closet that seemed to contain a couple of liquor bottles and an array of glasses. Seated in one of the chairs near a window was a gentleman reading a newspaper. He lowered the paper to see who had entered. Bill called out in recognition, "Harry, good morning. Let me introduce you to Doctor Henry Jones. Doctor Jones may be joining us here at the institutions." The gentleman set his paper down on the end table, removed his glasses placing them in his pocket, stood and walked towards us. "Henry, this is Doctor Harry Kimball. Harry, this is Doctor Jones." We shook hands, Bill informed Doctor Kimball that I was to be brought on board soon, as the full time physician for the prison.

Doctor Kimball smiled, "Please call me Harry. Will you be in residence here on the grounds, Henry?" I told him that Bill was kind enough to be showing me around, and that once my appointment was confirmed, I would be residing here. "Well, wonderful. We will be seeing a great deal of each other then. Bill, make sure you show him to apartment 210. He will get the morning sun there." Taking his pocket watch from his vest, Doctor Kimball said, "I hate to tell you man, you have missed the noon train back to Providence. Its thirty minutes past. I trust you didn't have any patients scheduled for this afternoon?" Bill told him that he had cleared his schedule for the day to meet with George and myself. He also wanted to tend to a couple of patients here, and would take the five o'clock back to Providence. Doctor Kimball took his jacket from the back of the chair and headed for the door. "Hope to be seeing you, Henry, and good luck with the General. He can be trying at times." Harry left, and we headed for the stairs leading to the second floor.

"Henry, I took the liberty of picking up the keys to two apartments from the personnel office. Why don't we look at 210 first, Harry seemed to think you would like it." We topped the stairs and turned right down the hallway. Reaching a door with brass numbers, 210. Bill reached into his pocket and took out several keys. He opened the door and stepped back allowing me to enter first. I was very impressed with what I saw. The parlor was larger than I had expected. It was furnished with two overstuffed chairs, each having a side table. A small roll top desk and with a chair was between two windows that looked out over the prison. Between the resident hall and the prison were the tracks for the Pawtuxet Valley branch of the New York Railroad. A large couch rested against the wall opposite the wall, with a sturdy oak table in front of it. The floor was covered by a worn, but serviceable oriental style carpet. I walked over to the desk and with a rumble opened it. I was surprised to see the desk already contained a supply of writing paper and envelopes. A fountain pen rested near the ink well. In the corner was a brass coat rack next to an empty china closet. I commented to Bill how impressed I was with what I saw. In the corner was a door, I assumed, lead to the bedroom. I opened it, Bill and I stepped in. Against the far wall was a large ornate Iron bed. The bare mattress appeared to be new. On both sides of the bed were small tables each with a matching oil lamp. At the foot of the bed was a large chest, opening it I found bedding neatly folded. The room also had two windows. From the right one I could see the Howard Train Depot. There were two wardrobes in the room one against the wall between the windows the other directly across from the first. Both were empty except for several wood and wire hangers. The highly polished maple floor had several small scatter rugs neatly placed about the room. "This is a beautiful apartment. This is much better than my place in Providence." I was told that the apartment was usually meant for a husband and wife. "Henry, why don't we take a look at the other apartment?" Bill locked the door behind us, and we walked down the hallway to a door numbered 201. This was located at the far end of the hall on the opposite side. There were several other door along the hallway, I assumed were other apartments. "The four corner apartments, are for full time physicians here at the institutions. Matter of fact, Harry lives in apartment 202 just across the hall. The other apartments are occupied by other staff members." I smiled to myself, I imagine the doctors got the best of the quarters. We entered 201, the parlor was very similar to the apartment we had just visited. The furniture was set in place exactly as the first. Again I thought, this is an institution, if it works in one, why change it. The main difference was in the bed room. The room had two beds of highly polished brass. They were each topped with, again, what appeared to be new mattresses. Looking out the windows. I could look up the hill upon other institutional buildings. Bill pointed out another brick building similar to this one, telling me that it was another residence hall for employees. Between the two buildings was a smaller one story building. I was told that this was the staff cafeteria. As a part of my benefits, I had full access for breakfast, lunch and dinner, seven days a week, free of charge. During the week, breakfast was served between 6:00am and 10:00am, lunch was from 12:00 noon to 2:00pm. Also, dinner was served from 5:00pm to 7:00pm. On Sunday, breakfast was served starting at 8:00am.

Bill commented. "Harry, is right. The other apartment does get the morning sun. The biggest drawback, is that the train passes by several times a day. The first morning train arrives at 5:00am. It could be disturbing to you. But, it does have a better view. The trees between the railroad tracks and the back wall of the prison are apple, peach, and cherry trees and they will be beautiful when they blossom next month." I continued my tour of the apartment, thinking how fortunate I am to be offered this position. Back home in England, a young doctor, such as myself, would not even be considered for an opportunity such as this, for many years. "Well, what do you think, Henry?" I turned to Bill with a grin from ear to ear.

"I think I would prefer apartment 210. I'm an early riser and I don't think the train will be a problem. What do you say Bill?" He smiled, and handed me the keys to 210, and welcomed me to the Institutions at Howard. I was surprised he handed me the keys. I still was not officially on the payroll, and I know there must be paper work to fill out at the personnel office. "Are you sure that it is alright to give me the keys? I still haven't been appointed officially."

"Don't worry, Henry. I'm sure the letter from the

Board will arrive at your Providence apartment buy the day after tomorrow. George has already given the head of personnel a heads up on your appointment. Iva Tweedy is in charge of the Personnel Office, she has been around here forever. She will take good care of you to get everything ready for you to start work here. She is a good person to get to know. Every employee here at the Institutions depends on her. She is a good person. We have time before she closes the office. We can take the other key back to her, I will introduce you to her." We locked the door to 201 and headed down the stairs and out the door. It was 1:45 as we walked up the hill and back to the building where I had met with Doctor Keene. The Personnel office was on the first floor, at the far end of the hall. The door was open, and we walked in. Behind the desk was heavy set women. She appeared to be in her early sixty's, with grey hair pulled back in a bun at the back of her head. She wore glasses that were perched at the end of her nose. "Iva, let me introduce you to Doctor Henry Jones. Henry, this is Mrs. Iva Tweedy, the brains behind everything here at the Facilities." The women smiled at Bill, and removed her glasses placing them on her desk. She stood, and gave a small curtsey, then reaching out her hand to greet me.

"Pleasure to meet you, Doctor." I took it and gave her a little bow. "I understand from Doctor Keene that you will be joining the staff here soon. Doctor McCaw told me that you will be in residence here. Have you selected your accommodations yet, doctor? I told her that

Bill was kind enough to show me what was available in the Residence Hall, and I had chosen apartment 210, if that was okay with her. Bill handed her back the keys to 201. She checked the tag on the keys to insure that the correct keys were returned. This was the first indication to me of how efficient and attentive she was in her job. "That is fine. So, you have the keys to 210?" I told her I did. She turned and opened a file cabinet and taking out a form. She wrote 210 on the line at the top, and my name. Placing the form on her desk she handed me a pen and asked me to sign it. "Feel free doctor, to move your belonging in at your leisure. Also, after you receive your letter of appointment from the Board stop back and see me. We have a few more papers to fill out acknowledging your employment, at that time I will have your meal card. You will need it to get your meals in the cafeteria." I signed, and handed her the pen and the form. She glanced at to make sure I had signed it correctly. Again, I thought, how impressed I was with Mrs. Tweedy and her attention to the details of her job. "Thank you, Doctor. I look forward to seeing you soon. I am sure you will enjoy your time here. My husband and I have lived and worked here for almost forty years. We raised our three children here. My husband Joshua, is in charge of the warehouse that supplies all the institutions." I told her, I hoped to meet him sometime. Bill chimed in, what a nice guy Josh was and can be a big help in expediting items needed in the facility.

"We have to be going." Bill told Mrs. Tweedy. "It's

getting late, and I would like to introduce Doctor Jones to Warden Viall before I have to leave for the 5:00 o'clock train." We said our good buys to Iva. As we left the Administration Building, I told Bill how impressed I was with Mrs. Tweedy. "She is a good women. She doesn't miss a trick, and has her thumb on everything and everyone who works here. She is the one person who, you might say, knows where all the bodies are buried." We both laughed.

We turned left at the end of the walkway and headed towards the prison. Across the street were freshly turned field. The smell of fertilizer was on the breeze that blew across the field. Bill pointed out that the fields to the north of the railroad tracks belonged to the prison, while those to south belonged to the Alms House and poor farm. To our left was an additional field. Bill informed me that this field was a matter of controversy between the Warden and the Administrator of the Alms House. Both claiming the field belongs to them. The claim was decided by the legislature in Providence. The Warden won the dispute. Some say because of his connections in the House. It never did settle well with the Alms House, and occasionally there is still problems over it. The prison stood large to our left after passing the field. The dome of the building was a prominent feature of the building. Reaching out from the dome to the north and the south were two wings containing the cell houses. The south was the Providence County Jail and the north wing was the designated the State Prison. In front of the main building stood a house with several tall chimneys. The front of the house had two stone pillar supporting a portal over the front door. The lawns in front of the prison were manicured with several trees strategically placed across the lawn. A walk way lead across the lawn, from the road to the front of the house. Both sides of the walk were cleared about two feet and appeared that they were readied for planting. We followed the walk to the house. Bill led me around the house to the right. We followed the building to the prison. Bill said, "The Warden should still be inside in his office." We turned left, under a stone archway, to the front door of the prison. We were greeted by a uniformed guard carrying a rifle. "Good afternoon, Doctor. And who would this be accompanying you today?" Bill introduced me as the new doctor who is being assigned to the prison. He told the officer that he wanted to introduce me to the Warden, and asked if he was still in his office. "Yes sir, I believe he is. Is he expecting you?" Bill indicated to the guard that he had told the Warden he planned to bring me around in the afternoon to introduce me. "Fine sir." The officer turned, cradling his rifle in his arms, he took a large key from his belt, turning it in the lock of the large metal door, he pushed the door open. "You know the way doctor. Have a good day." We entered and turned right ascending a steal staircase. At the top of the stairs to the left was a doorway, it was made of bars and had a large lock. Ahead of us was a large polished wooden door. A highly polished name plate read, Nelson Viall, Warden. The doorknob was also highly polished, so much so I could seem our reflections in it. I thought that more than impressive, the appearance of the doorway was intimidating. I could feel my heart rate increasing in my chest.

Bill knocked strongly on the heavy door. A voice from within call for us to come in. Bill opened the door and entered with me closely behind. In front of us sat a legend, General Nelson Viall.

He was seated behind a polished desk. At first glance the desk appeared to be facing the wrong way with drawers on the front. A closer look indicated the drawers were a façade, not functional. The four legs on the front of the desk were carved, as decorative as the face. In the center of the desktop was a diamond inlay, several shades darker than the wood of the rest of the desk, papers were neatly stacked in the upper right hand corner. Behind the desk, seated between the American Flag and the State Flag of Rhode Island, was a large man in a tie, vest and his shirt sleeves. His hair was graying and well-trimmed. Looking at his face, the most prominent feature were his eyes, they appeared dark and clear, almost as if he could see directly into you. His face was framed by bushy side-burns that ended near his chin. He stood before greeting us. Taking his suit jacket from the hanger in the corner, he put it on and buttoned it, after which he joined us in front of the desk. He shook Bill's hand, "Doctor McCaw good to see you. I assume that this is our new doctor."

The Warden took my hand and it disappeared within his grip. It was a strong grip. I suspect that he was being careful not to injure me as he closed his hand around mine. I could tell, he would be well able to crush it, had it been his intention. Bill made the introduction.

"Warden this is Doctor Henry Jones, he is being assigned to the Jail and the Prison as your fulltime physician. Doctor Jones this is Warden, General Nelson Viall." We continued our hand shake as the Warden took my right elbow into his left hand, drawing me in a little closer, looking me directly in the eyes. I told the Warden how nice it was to meet him and that I had heard a lot about him, and his service to the State.

"Well, I am a very fortunate man to have been able to serve this great state, over two wars and civilian service with the police and the prison." As he returned behind his desk to take his seat, he asked that we take a seat in the chairs in front of the desk. I mentioned that I had also heard that he had served in the State House of Representatives. The large man openly laughed, "Yes one term, not one of my shining endeavors. A number of my colleagues felt I had a problem compromising on some of the items appearing before us. The powers that be, felt that I could better serve by enforcing the laws rather than making them." Bill and I both smiled, knowing that with his reputation within the state and his service in the war, the people of the state would elect him as long as he wished to serve.

"Doctor McCaw, I'm sure that you are planning on bringing our new Physician up to speed on the work he will be doing here. You have been an asset to our operation here at the prison. As you know, I have been trying to get approval for a full time doctor to be assigned here for some time. I am sure that you had a great deal to do with the request being approved, and I thank you for that."

I may be young, but I knew that the Warden's compliments were kind, but strategic to indicate to me, that he and Bill had a good working relationship. And have been working together for the good of the operation. In truth, he didn't need help getting anything he wanted from the Board or the Legislature. Bill thanked him for the kind words, and echoed the positive effect having a full time doctor would be. "Will you have time today to show Doctor Jones around the prison? I am sure he would want to take a look at our hospital, and tour our facility." Bill indicated that we had to make the 5:00 o'clock train, and it was now after 3:30.

"I'm sure that you can find time another day before Doctor Jones officially begins his assignment here. I would like to introduce you to my command staff. My Deputy Warden and my shift command people are available before you gentlemen depart."

The General stood and went to a file cabinet, and took out a piece of paper. "Before you leave, Doctor Jones, I need to give you a copy of the rules and regulations that the prisoners have to abide by. You should understand that we have about 190 sentenced prisoners, and approximately 300 men in the jail wing. These are generally men who are not accustomed to following directions and rules. If they were they would not find themselves in prison. Many of them have had this problem from childhood. They couldn't follow rules placed upon them by their parents, or school, not to mention society. With that in mind, it is most important that I establish rules and guidelines for their behavior while they reside here. The rules are strictly enforced by all staff, to include yourself and other non-custodial employees. As Doctor McCaw will, I'm sure, confirm, individuals who are new to working within a prison can be a target for prisoners, who would attempt to garner sympathy for their plight, a condition that they have brought upon themselves. I do not expect that you would take direct action with the prisoner, but you must report violations to an officer or supervisory staff."

The Warden handed me the copy of the rules across the desk, and sat back down. He interlocked his fingers with his hands atop of this head and leaned back into his chair. Giving me time to read the list. I looked at the list of rules and regulations for prisoners. He may have been expecting a reaction from me. But I offered none.

RULES AND REGULATIONS FOR PRISONERS

1. When the corridor bells firs ring in the morning, each prisoner shall rise, dress, make up his bed, put his cell in order, and be ready to leave the cell at the sound of the signal bell. Upon returning to his cell he is required to close the

door and stand at it until counted.

2. No prisoner shall have in his cell any pen, ink, pencil, or other writing material, or tools of any kind without the permission of the Warden.

3. Prisoners shall not write or draw upon or in any way deface their cells. They shall keep their persons, cell, and everything pertaining thereto perfectly neat and clean. They shall not make over, alter, or destroy their clothing. Before leaving their cells at any time they shall first put them in good order.

4. Every prisoner is forbidden to read aloud, talk, sing, or make any unnecessary noise whatever at any time, either in his cell or elsewhere. At half past 8 o'clock in the evening each and every prisoner shall go to bed, and shall not get up therefrom until the ringing of the morning bell, unless compelled to do so by necessity. They shall not put food, clothing, or reading matter in the slop bucket.

5. Prisoners will approach the officers, in a respectful manner, and all communications between them and the officers must be as brief as possible.

6. They shall not converse or communicate in any way with one another, nor shall they, without the permission of the Warden, upon any pretense whatsoever, speak to or communicate with any person not connected with the institution. In

the Sunday school, however, they may converse with their teachers upon religious subjects only, and on one Sunday in each month they may speak in free religious conference. Those whose behavior is unexceptionable may, by permission of the Warden, talk with one another at table in the mess room.

7. They shall not leave their work or place where they may be stationed without permission of the officer having them in charge, nor shall they gaze at visitors, officers, or other persons. Their attention shall be given wholly to their work.

8. They shall work diligently and in silence on week days. They shall pay respectful attention whenever religious services are held and when entertainments are given for their instruction or amusement, and they shall not deface or in any way injure books or papers which may be given them to read.

9. The clergy of the Protestant churches and of the Roman Catholic Church have the privilege of imparting religious instructions and of administering their rights and sacraments on Sundays, and the attendance of the inmates at the services to be in no case compulsory.

10. Inmates of the jail may be visited by their relatives and friends once in four weeks, and inmates of the prison once in three months. Visits

must be made by the relatives and friends of any one prisoner at the same time. Under special circumstances visits may be made oftener by permission of the Warden. The law relative to the State Prison contains this clause, "No convict shall receive anything but the prison allowance, unless by order of the physician."

11. These rules do not apply to persons imprisoned for debt, or awaiting trial, or held as witnesses. The conduct of such persons, however, must always be orderly, quiet, and in strict conformity with the rules of the institution.

12. The behavior of every prisoner must always be orderly, quiet, and in strict conformity with the rules of the institution.

13. Every violation of the foregoing rules and every act detrimental to the maintenance of good order and discipline will be considered a reason for punishment.

14. Prisoners who choose to labor, although not required by law to do so, must, when at work, obey the foregoing rules.

"Take the rules with you, doctor, look them over and if you have any questions I am always available to you. Now, why don't we go down stairs and meet some of the staff, before you gentlemen have to depart."

We stood and headed for the office door. I looked back and saw the Warden take a black pistol from the center draw of the desk and put into his pocket. He locked the door to the office and we descended the iron stairs that we had climbed earlier. At the bottom of the stairs we turned right. Before us was a barred door. Several uniformed officers were on the other side. One came and unlocked the door blocking our entrance. The guard opening the door gave a smart salute, greeting the Warden with a cordial, "Good afternoon, Sir." The Warden returned the salute and the greeting. We found ourselves in a wide hallway with several barred doors.

The General pointed to our right. "This is the Committing Room, all new prisoners are processed here for both the jail and the prison. They are searched, showered and uniformed, before being assigned to their cells."

The next door was solid metal with a small six inch window. I looked through it and saw another barred door about eight feet away. "This is the entrance into the prison cell blocks." Directly across from this door on the other side of the large hallway, was a replica of the door I had just peered through. The warden commented, "Through that door is the Jail wing."

Walking a short distance to the right was a small office. Seated at the desk was a tall slender man in uniform. His uniform was trimmed with a double row the brass buttons, on his chest was a gold colored badge. He stood to greet us and his boss. "Gentlemen, I'd like to introduce you to Edmund Slocum. Ed is the shift overseer, he is the man in charge of our morning shift. Ed, you know Doctor McCaw, and this gentleman is Doctor Henry Jones. Doctor Jones is new to the institutions and is being assigned as our full time doctor. So, you will be seeing a great deal of each other. Edmund and I go way back. He is the son of my old commanding officer. His father was killed at Bull Run. He was a good commander." We greeted one another and the General walked us across the hall to another office.

Seated at the desk was a younger man in a brown suit. I noticed the right sleeve of the jacket had shades of black ink smudges from the cuff to the elbow. On the desk in front of him was a large book, he was intently writing in. The gentleman was so intent on his work, he didn't notice us at the door of the office. "Good afternoon Frank." The man looked up with a start, and stood up from his chair. He apologized for not noticing us. "Gentlemen, let me introduce you to Frank Viall, Frank is our clerk. He keeps track of all our inmates, commitments, and dates of release. Also keeps the debtors log, and tracks all our expenses and income. He is the real brains of the prison." The man smiled, pleased with the compliment from his boss. "Frank you know Doctor McCaw. Let me introduce you to Doctor Henry Jones. Doctor Jones will be our new full time Physician." We shook hands and greeted each other. "Before you ask. Yes, Frank is a relative. He is my nephew, my Brother John's boy. He is very good at his job and, after all, this is Rhode Island and it is somewhat of a tradition to surround yourself with people you know and can trust." We all laughed. I really did understand. In my time living in the state, I had noticed this phenomenon through government and industry. It is a small state and everyone seems to know everyone else.

We walked across the hall, down a short corridor to a wooden door. The Warden knocked, without waiting, he opened the door and we walked in. "How are things going today, Deputy?" He answered confirming all is well. "Deputy, I would like to introduce you to Doctor Henry Jones. He is being assigned here as our full time doctor. Doctor, this is my Deputy Warden Alonzo Bowe." The Deputy stood and reach across his desk to shake hands.

The office was larger than the other offices we had been in. There were several barred window in the office. One behind the desk and three more along the wall. They overlooked the prison yard. Looking out I could see the main gate into the yard, and two guard towers, one at the main gate and the other in the far corner. There were two or three prisoners in the yard, standing on the wall was an armed guard watching their activity. I commented on the view. Smiling, the Warden said. "The Deputy likes to keep an eye on what is going on and wants the inmates to know that he is always watching." The Deputy smiled back at him.

All of a sudden I heard a loud bell ringing. It was

coming from the prison yard. I was nervous that there may be a problem. The Warden put his hand on my shoulder, telling me to relax, that it was the bell signaling the end of the inmates work day. Bill pulled out his pocket watch, opening it he said that it was 4:00 o'clock and that if we were going to make the train back to Providence we had to get going.

The Howard Depot was a good stretch of the legs from the prison. The Warden told Bill that we could cut through the orchard behind the wall, and by crossing the tracks at that point we would be close to the depot. He warned us to make sure we waved to the tower guards so they would recognize us.

Bill was well known to all the staff. When I glanced out the window as we were leaving, I saw a group of inmates walking in single file towards the prison wing. They were followed by an officer and the guards in the towers were visible standing on the wall with their rifles in hand.

Doctor McCaw and I bid our goodbyes, thanking the Warden for taking the time to introduce me to his staff. As we exited the Deputy Warden's Office, Bill pointed to a barred door to the left. "This leads to the mess hall. The prisoners enter from the two doors in the corridor from the housing units of the jail and the prison.

If we had time, I would show you the kitchen and introduce you to Bill Towne, he is the Steward, and runs an excellent kitchen. He has several handpicked prisoners that work for him. Once a month you will have to inspect the kitchen and report its condition to the Warden. The last thing the boss wants to have is to have the men come down with sickness from bad food or un-sanitary conditions. I have never found a problem in the last two years, so it is really just a routine in place to make sure all is well."

We reached the outer heavy door, Bill pounded upon it and I could hear the key turning in the lock. It was pulled open, and we walked out. A strange feeling of freedom swept over me. Even though I knew that I was able to leave whenever I chose to.

We turned left and walked down the walkway in front of the prison wing. In front of us was a stone carriage house and stable, where the Warden's horse and buggy were kept. As we got closer, to our left was the large metal doors to enter the prison yard. I could see that above the center of the double doors was a wheel with a screw. I was told that this was how the doors were secured.

On the other end of the facility there was a matching door to enter the jail yard. We walk about twenty five feet away from the wall so we would be in full view of the guards on the towers. Bill yell up to the man in the tower closest to the gate. He came out of the tower, waved and yelled back to Bill to have a good evening. He then waived to the other guard further down the wall acknowledging that we were allowed to pass along the wall. We crossed the tracks and went up a small incline turning right towards the train depot.

When we climbed up onto the train platform, it was 4:40pm. Bill and I stood talking as several more passengers began gathering on the platform heading home from their work. "Well, Henry what do you think?" I told him that I was very impressed with everything I had seen. "How about the General. He is quite a character isn't he?" I told him that I was very impressed by him and that he projected strength and leadership. Also, I felt a little intimidated by his presence. Bill smiled. "He is quite a man. His staff would follow his lead anywhere." I gave out a little laugh, telling him, I think I would also.

The train arrived in a cloud of smoke and steam, and we boarded one of the cars. We found seats together and continued to talk about our day. We discussed getting together on Saturday for dinner. Bill offered to pick me up around two in the afternoon and take me to a men's club that he belonged to in Pawtucket. The club's name was, The To Kalon Club. Its membership, most of Irish decent, consists of the most prominent men in government and industry in the state.

The train arrived at the Providence station and we parted ways heading home. I have a lot to do before I begin work. Gathering and boxing up my belongings to move to Howard. I smiled to myself, I hope that I am not being premature in readying myself for my new job. After all I haven't even received my letter of appointment from the Board. I'm still getting used to how things are done here in Rhode Island. The state seems to work on a more personal level than "official level". I am sure that good Doctor McCaw will fill me in a lot more at dinner on Saturday.

CHAPTER 3

The Wait

In my apartment on Friendship Street, I slept like a baby. My live seems as if it is coming together. I have made a number of new friends here in Rhode Island. The interview went well, and it appears that I have secured a full time position with the State as the prison doctor. I can't help but thinking that something might go wrong. Until I get the letter of appointment from the Board of Charities and Corrections, I still harbor concerns that everything that took place yesterday was all very premature. I must just stop thinking about it, and trust that Doctor Keene and Bill know what is happening and everything will be fine. Even the General seemed to be on board with me working within his facility.

I have to go see my landlady this morning and tell her that I will be leaving soon so that she can begin finding a new tenant for the apartment. I will see if she has some boxes I can use to pack up my books and other belongings. There is my trunk in the basement that I used when I traveled here on the ship from South Hampton, I can begin packing my clothes. Maybe I will stop by the post office to see if there is any mail. I smiled to myself. Calm down, the interview was only Tuesday. It is way too soon to have a letter from the Board, it was only yesterday. It is an exciting time in my life.

On my way to the basement, I stopped and knocked on the landlady's door. "Who is it? One moment." The door swung open.

"My goodness, good morning Doctor Jones. What can I do for you?

I informed her that, it appears that I would be leaving for a position in Cranston. That I would be working at the institutions, and in residence there.

"Do you know when you will be moving, doctor?"

I told her that it would be soon and that I wanted to let her know so she would be able to find a new tenant. I offered to pay the rent for April, as today was March 29th and I didn't want to inconvenience her, leaving her without a tenant, and no rent coming in.

"Thank you Doctor. On your last day we will work out the rent for the month. I should have no problem renting the apartment. I will post it at Brown. There are always students or faculty in need of accommodations." I ask her if she had any boxes or crates that I may use to begin packing. "I'm not sure. But should you find any in the basement feel free to make use of what you may need. I don't get down to the basement often and don't really remember what I have down there."

"Will you be needing a man to help transport your belonging to your new residence? My nephew, Burt, has a transport business. I'm sure he could give you a good price on such a short move. If you are interested I will have him come by and you gentlemen can work out the cost." I thanked her and started down into the basement. I was wondering on how I would get my things to Howard. Shipping them by train would be expensive for such a short distance, and once at the depot, I would still need to get them to the residence hall.

There in the corner was my steamer trunk. I looked around the basement and found four wooden crates. They appeared to be old vegetable crates made of wooden slats and wire. They would be perfect for my books. It took me three trips up and down the stairs to bring the trunk and the crates to my apartment. I laughed at myself as I sat in the easy chair to rest. I am not use to physical labor.

I looked into my wardrobe and took stock on what clothing I had. I owned two suits and five dress shirts. With having to wear a suit and tie every day, I will be needing at least one more suit, a couple more dress shirts and ties. My father used to tell me as I was growing up, that a man needed only two suits. One for wearing and one for burying. I can wait to purchase any other items until I begin to receive my salary. After lunch I will stop at Brooks Brothers. They have a good selection of ready-made men's suits, and a tailor to make any adjustments needed.

I left my apartment and walked down the street to College Hill. I always felt sorry for the horses pulling a carriage or wagon up this steep hill. I reached the bottom and walked over the bridge into the main part of the city. A short walk down Weybosset Street was the Arcade. The building was unique it had an entrance on both sides of the building. One on Weybosset Street and the other on Westminster Street, just past the Turks Head Building. The building housed several small businesses, a dress shop, a small restaurant, and several specialty shops.

The restaurant was on the street level, I went in and took a seat near the entrance. I enjoyed watching the people as they went about their lives. Eating alone, as I generally did, this was part of my entertainment. The waitress took my order, a chicken sandwich and a bowl of the soup of the day, onion, and a cup of tea. I watched the passersby and thought that it was particularly busy for mid-week early afternoon.

A police officer was standing across the street. I had remembered that the General was once the chief of police. Dr. McCaw, mentioned on the train ride that Warden Viall, when he became warden took the best of the Providence Police with him when he left. I watched as the policeman stood twirling his baton, first to the front then it spun behind him. He was very proficient and quite entertaining. My lunch arrived. The soup was very good. It warmed my insides. My walk from my apartment was quite brisk. The March wind was cold, even though the air temperature was in the fifties. I am trying to decide if I should stop at the post office after I go to Brooks Brothers. I think I will wait until tomorrow. To go today, would most likely be a wasted trip. I finished my tea and paid my bill. The lunch special was thirty five cents, another nickel tip and I was on my way.

Walking down Westminster Street to the Brooks Brothers Shop, the wind was strong. The building of the city created a wind tunnel, the front of my overcoat was blowing open. Several times I just caught my hat before it blew off my head.

I reached the shop, and climbed the two steps and entered. The store was paneled with a warm maple wood. Several racks held a variety of suits in various colors on tables there were shirts on display and another had a number of ties. Towards the back of the store were three racks of overcoats alongside was another table with several styles of hats. I walked to the racks where the suits were displayed. A clerk came walking over.

"Good afternoon, sir. May I be of assistance?" I informed him that I was in need of a suit. He assisted me in removing my overcoat and suit jacket. The clerk hung up my clothing with great care. "May I gather a few measurements sir?" He removed a yellow tape measure from around his neck, and began to take measurements of my shoulders, arms, waist and chest. "Did you have anything special in mind, sir? I told him that I was starting a new position that would require me to be attired in a suit daily. I mentioned that I already had two fine suits but would need another or maybe two more.

"I see. You are wearing a very fine suit today." He picked up my jacket and examined it. "I see this is a custom made. Made in London, I see." I told him it was a gift from my father upon my graduation from medical school. "Very nice Doctor. We have a good selection of pre-made suits, for daily use. Each comes with a matching vest, you may be interested in. We also have a custom department should you prefer."

I informed the clerk that I needed suits that would be serviceable, wear well and I would be needing them within the week, if that was possible. "That would not pose a problem. I have several in your size to choose from." He directed me to my size on the rack. I slid the hangers along the rack taking a look at each. Removing a brown one I laid it across the rack. "May I assist you?" The clerk removed the jacket from its hanger and helped me into it.

I looked at myself in the mirror. I smiled, and thought, what a fine looking chap. The clerk brushed out my shoulders and ran his fingers down the seam of the sleeves. "We can shorten the sleeves a little, but other than that it is a fine fit, sir." I asked what the price would be. The clerk removed a small note pad from his pocket. "This suit will be fifteen dollars and comes with a matching vest." I removed the jacket, the clerk helped me place it back on the hanger. He set it aside, as I fingered my way through the rack of other suites my size. I came upon a blue suit with a pin stripe. The material was a lighter weight that the brown one. "This item just came in. It is our summer weight. This unit does not come with a vest, however it does come with two pair of trousers. We are able to custom make you a matching vest if you would like."

The clerk helped me try on the jacket. It was very comfortable, almost as if I had no jacket on at all. I looked at myself again in the mirror. It is a nice change from what I have been wearing. All my other suits were of a heaver material a wool blend. Living in England, warm weather was short lived. A suit such as this would be very impractical. I asked what the cost of this item would be. "Let me look it up for you, sir. This model just arrived and I don't have the cost down." While the clerk check on the price, I held up both suits, inspecting them. The sales clerk returned carrying a slip of paper. "Sorry Doctor for the wait. I spoke to the manager and this item is thirteen dollars and seventy five cents. I was informed if you were to purchase both items, we would be able to work with you on a special price." I told the salesman that I intended on also purchasing a couple of shirts and ties. I noticed his eyes light up. I imagined that he worked on commission, and he must have thought that he had made his salary on just one customer today. "I believe we can reach a satisfactory agreement on the transaction. The gentleman went over to the manager and spoke to him. He returned with the manager and I was invited into his office.

The manager introduced himself as did I. "My clerk informs me that you are interested in making several purchases. Doctor, here at Brooks Brothers we have special concierge program for gentleman who have special needs for men's furnishings. We keep a file with sizes and particular styles of items you prefer. All is quite confidential, and one of our sales people will be assigned to assist you with any needs you may have. Our special clients also receive special discounts on many items." I thought for a moment on how convenient that would be, seeing that I would be living outside the city. I thanked him and told him I thought that an arraignment such as he suggested would work well seeing that I would soon be relocating to Cranston and working at the State Institutions. "We have several gentlemen who presently work there that are our clients. Do you have a special employee here at Brooks Brothers you would prefer as your concierge?"

I told the manager that the gentleman who was assisting me today seemed to be very competent. "Very well. Johnathan will be your man here at Brooks Brothers." The manager summonsed the clerk to the office and informed him of my decision. Johnathan thanked me for my confidence in him and assured me he would do all he could to assist me with my needs. We shook hands and continued shopping for what I needed. When I was done, I had purchased two suites, three new shirts with collars and cuffs, and several pair of socks. The bill totaled thirty eight dollars and thirty cents. The total after Johnathan figured the discount was thirty five dollars and fifty cents. It was a little more than I had planned on spending today. But everything I purchased was needed. I paid the salesman and began getting ready to leave. I was putting my jacket and overcoat on, when Johnathan walked over to me. He placed a new derby hat on my head which fit perfectly.

"Not today Johnathan, maybe the next time." The clerk smiled and told me that the derby was on him, and would be delivered with the other items on Friday to my Friendship Street address. He thanked me for trusting him to take care of my clothing needs. "You're a fine man Johnathan, I thank you for all your help today. I am sure we will see each other again soon."

I headed out the door and on to Westminster Street. The wind had died down a bit, and it was a much more pleasant walk back to my apartment. By the time I reached Collage Hill I was actually quite warm. I removed my overcoat, carrying it over my arm I started my climb up to Benefit Street. A right on Benefit leads me to my apartment on Friendship.

I arrived home and as I ascended the stairs my land-lady opened her door and told me that her nephew Burt, was here, if I would like to speak to him about moving my belonging to my new apartment in Cranston. "Yes, yes indeed. Just let me put my coat upstairs and I will be right back down." She told me don't bother, that she would send him up to see me. I entered my apartment and hung up my coat and jacket. A knock at the door, it was Burt. I opened the door to see a large man who appeared to be in his early thirties. He reached out his hand and introduced himself. His hand was large and rough. A working man's hand.

"Aunty Helen said you needed help moving your belonging to the Institutions in Howard. If you would like I could take care of that for you. I can give you a good price, you being a friend of my aunt's and all." I asked Burt to take a seat, so we could talk. "How much stuff will need to be moved?" He asked. I pointed out to him my large steamer trunk and all my books that were still on my bookshelves waiting to be packed up. I told him that I wanted to go through the books to see what I wanted to take with me, and which ones I was going to get rid of.

"When do you think you will be ready to move?" I told him that Friday would be good for me. That would give me the weekend to settle into my new residence.

All the time I'm thinking how fast this is all happening. I haven't even received my letter of appointment. I asked Burt How much he would you charge me for the move.

"I will pack up your books, you take care of packing

your clothing and other personal items. I will load my wagon and take your things to Cranston and place them in your new apartment. Upstairs I imagine?" I smiled that's correct. "I can do this job by myself, I won't need to hire a man. How does three dollars cash money sound?" I told Burt that sounded more than fair to me. We shook hands again, deal is struck. I asked him if he needed me to give him something up front. "No, no Doctor. We can settle up when the job is done. I will be here, and get started by 8:00am on Friday. I should have you all settled in your new place by the afternoon." I thanked him and wished him a good day.

I started looking through the books on the shelves. There were quite a few medical books that I would be taking with me. I had a two books containing a collection of Edgar Allen Poe's works. One with short stories, the other with poems. He was a strange fellow. I have been told that he resided here in Providence for a period of time and dated a local women. Things didn't work out between them, alcohol seemed to be the cause of the difficulty between them. I also have several books by Dickens, which I brought with me from home, in England. It was Dickens who started me on my pursuit to treat the poor and forgotten of our society. My copies of the Adventures of Tom Sawyer also The Adventures of Huckleberry Finn, by Mark Twain are an easy read and I will most likely read many times. Well, this isn't going to get me anywhere. I need to part with some of these books. I will box up what I am sure

I don't want and find a place to donate them to. Maybe the Providence Library or a school would enjoy receiving them. I will think on it and check around in the morning. Today was a very productive day.

I awoke to a lovely morning. The sun was streaming though my bedroom window. A look outside confirmed a beautiful day sunny and spring like. Rhode Island does have very changeable weather. Yesterday cool windy and damp today, pleasant and clear. I lit the burner on my gas stove and put the pot on for tea. Opening the bread box I had a piece of cornbread left I thought would be nice for breakfast. A walk to the post office is on my agenda for today. With any luck, they may have my letter of appointment. That would make my day. The library is near the post office. I will stop in to see if they take donations.

A knock came from my door. I opened the door and standing there was my landlady. She was holding a jar of something.

"I heard you stirring around, Doctor. Would you like a jar of blackberry jam? I put it up myself and still have several jars left." I thanked her and took the jar. I told her how fortunate I was. I was just sitting down for breakfast and the jam would be wonderful on my cornbread.

"I don't want to keep you from your breakfast Doctor Jones. But I do want to thank you for hiring Burt to move your belonging. He really can use the money, he will do a good job." I told her that I was sure he would. I thought it was a good time to raise the issue of the rent for April.

"Burt will be moving most of my belonging tomorrow. I will be keeping back a few clothes I will need until I get completely moved in my new apartment. I was hoping that I could stay a few days into April. I am willing to give you the whole rent for the month." She told me that she had already posted the apartment at Brown and was waiting for any takers. She told me that if I were to give her April's rent and someone wanted to move in during part of the month she would return any excess to me. I told her, "Don't worry about it. You have been a wonderful landlady and you can keep anything extra you may receive from a new rental. Won't you join me in a cup of tea?" She declined and told me she had to get back to her house work. "Thank you again for the jam." She smiled and left to return down stairs.

I finished my breakfast and made ready for my walk to the Post Office and the Library. Such a beautiful morning I had no need for my overcoat. Down the stairs I bounded and on to Friendship Street. I had a spring in my step today with the hope of receiving my letter of appointment.

I crossed the Providence River Bridge and headed over to Washington Street. The library would be opening by the time I arrived. I entered the building and went directly to the main desk. "Excuse me, I was wondering if the Library accepted book donations?" I have several books by Dickens, Poe and Mark Twain, plus a number of others, should you be interested." She smiled and asked if I was sure I wanted to part with them. "I am in the process of moving from Providence to Cranston and I have quite a collection of books. I thought it would be a good opportunity to thin out my collection." I asked if they could have someone pick them up at my apartment tomorrow. I gave her my address and said that I would be there all morning. I was told that one of their volunteers would be by around ten on Friday morning. The women thanked me again, and I was on my way to Weybosset Street to the Post Office.

I approached one of the postal clerks who was standing behind one of a half dozen caged windows. "Good morning Sir. My name is Doctor Henry Jones from Friendship Street. Do I have any mail today?" I was told that he would check. He slipped from the stool he was seated on, returning in about two minutes holding three envelopes. The clerk took a second look at the name and address to make sure he all the letters were indeed mine. He slid them through the opening in the cage to me. He commented that one was from overseas. "From my family, I'm sure. Thank you and have a good day."

I took the letters and sorted them in my hand, looking for one from the State of Rhode Island. There in the corner of one of the envelopes was the anchor and banner "Hope", the State Seal. I rushed to the counter that ran against the wall, running my finger across the opening of the sealed envelope tearing it open. I unfolded the letter, my heart was beating fast. The letterhead confirmed it was from the State Board of Charities and Corrections.

"Dear Doctor Henry Jones,

It is with great pleasure that the Board of Charities and Corrections, are able to offer you a permanent appointment to State Service. You are being assigned to the Medical Services Section of the State Institutions at Howard, Rhode Island. Your starting salary is $750.00 per year, to be paid on the first of each month, beginning April 1, 1893. In addition you are granted housing privileges in the residence hall of the institutions and dining privileges. Your regular hours are thirty five hours per week. You are allowed ten days paid leave during the year, with the approval of the Superintendent of Medical Services.

Your immediate supervisor will be Superintendent Doctor George F. Keene, M.D. It is the understanding of the Board of Charities and Corrections that your initial assignment will be as Physician for the Rhode Island State Prison and the Providence County Jail.

At your earliest convince report to Mrs. Iva Tweedy in the Personnel Office, in the Administration Building, at Howard to complete paper work, and be assigned your housing benefits.

Again, Congratulations from the Board of Charities and Corrections, and welcome to service of the State of

Rhode Island and Providence Plantations.

Sincerely Yours;

Honorable Thomas Coggeshall, Chairman of the Board

The weight of the world has just been lifted from my shoulders. I stuffed all three letters into my breast pocket. I will read them back at my apartment later. Out the Post Office I went. My mind racing with everything I still had to do. First things first. I'm stopping for a drink at the pub on the way back to my apartment.

I almost forgot the letter I received from England. I sat down at my desk and tore open the envelope. It was from my parents. All is well, my mother and father were concerned that they had not received word from me on how I was managing in America in quite some time. I felt terrible to have left them worrying about me. But I had little to tell them. I wanted to wait until I had a secure position in my profession. I do have a few private patients, but not enough to actually call it my own practice. I must write them with the good news. There is no time like the present.

Another beautiful morning. Not just the morning sun shining through my bedroom window, but a feeling of great peace and accomplishment. My life in America is becoming settled. The letter I wrote last evening, will bring my parents great peace of mind, that my move was a good one for me. I need to get a move on. Burt will be arriving soon. I put the tea kettle on and got myself ready for the day. I will mail the letter to my parents from the Howard Post Office. I think the post mark will be a good omen for myself and them.

A knock at my door, brought my mind back from day dreaming of my future. I opened the door and as expected there was Burt. "Good morning Burt. It appears to be a beautiful day outside today." Burt confirmed that it was indeed. Sunny and cool, a day perfect to move. "How would you like a cup of tea?"

We were interrupted by another knock at the door. I went to the door and there was a young man standing there. "Good morning, young man. How may I help you?" He told me was sent by the library to secure a donation of books. "Oh, yes. I had forgotten that you were coming today." I opened one of the several boxes I had packed up to insure I was giving him the correct box.

"Here you go. I hope they will be a good addition to the selections offered by the library." The young man thanked me and was on his way.

The water was ready and Burt and I sat over our tea and discussed the move. I would be riding with him to Howard on his wagon. I told him that I had to do paper work and other things to take care of and would not be returning with him. I planned to take the train back to Providence at the end of the day.

"Well Burt, I think we should get started." I grabbed the appointment letter in case Mrs. Tweedy needed to see it. And, Burt and I started bringing the boxes to his wagon. He didn't think I should be helping. He told me, it was his job and I was his employer and shouldn't be carrying the boxes. Taking my steamer trunk by the handle on one end, he swung it up to his shoulder. I laughed. "You are quite a man, Burt. I had a problem dragging the trunk into the parlor." We laughed together. I held the door open for him, and he loaded the wagon. As we turned to go back upstairs, I heard my name being called. It was the salesman from Brooks Brothers.

He had my order, two large boxes with the company's name printed on them, tied together with string. "Just on time. We are loading my belonging to take them to my new residences. You can just put the boxes in the wagon, thank you very much." We shook hands and I told him we would be seeing each other again. Burt had already gone back upstairs for more of my boxes.

I saw a police officer walking up the street, spinning his baton. He called out a good morning. "Good morning officer." He inquired about what was happening. "I am in the process of moving to my new address in Cranston. I have just been employed as the permanent Physician for the Jail and Prison." He smiled and told me to give his regards to the General, and went on to tell me how it was the General had helped him get on to the police force. "I have to get back to loading the wagon." The officer said that he would stand by the wagon to insure that no one took my belonging while I was up stairs.

Burt and I finished loading the wagon. I made sure I left enough clothing for myself. I had planned to stay in the city a few more days to finish up some business. I had a few patients that I was treating and I wanted to tell them I would not be able to continue as their doctor. I plan to recommend Bill to them. It would be an easy transfer and I will still be in contact with him to ensure a smooth transfer. Climbing up on the wagon and we were off. We turned north on Benefit Street. By going to the end we will be able to avoid College Hill, and head south again on Fountain Street and head out of the city.

In just over an hour we arrived at the Howard complex. I directed Burt to the residence hall, and the team and wagon pulled up in front of the building. "Quite a view of the prison, Doctor. I always get a chill whenever I look at the place." I said that I agreed but in a way it is a beautiful building, a reminder of the old castles back in England.

Burt unloaded the wagon. I held the door. When he was done. I thanked him and handed him his pay. "There is a little something extra for you Burt, for carry me along with my belongings." He asked if I would be going back with him. "I will be taking the evening train back to Providence. I have some paper work to do at the personnel office and I wanted to start to get my belonging put away." Burt climbed up on to the wagon, waved good bye. The horse's hooves I could still hear after they were out of sight.

A quick glance at my pocket watch told me I should be off to the personnel office to meet with Mrs. Tweedy. I walked up to the main road and crossed the street to the Administration Building. Walking down the hall my footsteps echoed down the hallway. I turned into the office and there at her desk was Mrs. Tweedy. She looked up over her glasses. "Ah Doctor Jones. I take it that you received your letter of appointment?" I told her that it had just arrived yesterday, and I had come, as instructed, to her to do whatever paper work was needed. She stood and went to her file cabinet, and removed a folder. As she placed it on her desk I noticed on the tab it said Henry Jones, Doctor. She opened it and thumbed through the papers, taking out two of them. "I see you have already received your key and signed the agreements on housing and dining. Here is your dining card for the staff dining room." Iva handed me a card that was already printed with my name and my residence apartment number. "I must inform you that our pay schedules run from Friday thru Thursday. Today is the first day of the pay period for April, even though it is only March 31st. Today will be your first official day of employment.

We will give your first week as time to get settled and moved it and acquainted with the grounds. You will need to touch base with Doctor Keene and the General this coming week and be ready to actually start at the prison by next Friday the 7th. I'm sure you already know that your salary is $750.00 per year, and is payable every two week. That is $31.25 each payday. Any additional hours you are required to work will be signed off by Dr. Keene and will be paid on the off pay week. Do you have any questions, Doctor?" I told her that I understood. "Wonderful, just sign these two papers and you are all set. Your first payday will be the 14th of April. Would you prefer receiving it here at my office or would you like it sent over to the prison?" I told her that here would be fine as I had to walk by the Administration Building on my way back to the residence hall every day. I thanked Iva for all her help and said good bye.

On my way back to the residence hall, I stopped at the dining room for lunch. It was just after one in the afternoon. I hadn't eaten all day, only a cup of tea before loading the wagon. Being a little late in the afternoon for lunch, I had a cup of coffee, a bowel of clam chowder with bread and butter. I showed my meal card and was welcomed by the worker. She had mentioned that she had not seen me before. I told her that I will be living on the grounds and she would be seeing a lot of me.

I still had time before the 5:00 o'clock train back to Providence so I returned to the residence hall and started organizing my belongings. My thoughts were darting all over. So much to do, so many new experiences to come, and so much to learn. Not to mention, how would my relationship be with the Warden. Everyone has been telling me how much they respect him, but on the other hand, how difficult he can be to work with.

I walked to the train depot. On the way there I walked past the back wall of the prison, thinking that soon I would be on the other side of the wall, looking out. I laughed to myself, at least I could leave when I wanted.

Saturday morning, I stepped out to pick up the morning Journal. When I got to the bottom of the stairs the landlady opened her door.

"Good morning, Doctor. How did the move go? I trust that my nephew took good care of you." I assured her that Burt did a fine job and thanked her for recommending him to me. When I returned with the paper, I put the pot on for some tea. I planned for a quiet morning looking forward to going to dinner with Bill McCaw. He told me he would pick me up in his carriage for the ride to Pawtucket.

I dressed in one of my new suits. I had heard that the To Kalon Club was very exclusive and I didn't want to embarrass Bill by showing up as his guest dressed shabbily. I looked at my watch as I slipped it into my vest pocket. It was 1:45, Bill should be arriving soon. I left the apartment and went to wait for him out front of the apartment. As I reached the sidewalk, was greeted by the same police officer I had met yesterday.

"A fine afternoon, Doctor. You look like you are going somewhere special all dress up as you are." I commented on how observant he was and yes I did have special plans for the afternoon with Doctor McCaw. "Oh, what a fine man Doctor McCaw. He is my family's physician. A fine Doctor he is. Not to say you're not, but I know his work. He tended my daughter. We thought we were going to lose her. He did tell us later that he thought we may lose her also."

Just then Bill pulled up in his carriage. "Hello, Doctor McCaw!" Bill greeted the policeman, asking how he and the family was. "Fine, fine Doctor all is well. You Doctors have a good rest of the day. I have to be getting on with my beat." I climbed into the carriage and we were off.

We arrived at the club. It was a large brick building with two white pillars at the door way. On the side of the building was a large carriage house with a stable. Bill parked his carriage, and a man was there to take charge of the carriage and horse. We entered the club. Inside was richly paneled in dark wood. Several leather easy chairs were placed around the large room. About a half dozen men were seated about, some smoking cigars with a drink in hand. Others were engaged in conversations. When we entered we drew the attention of several gentlemen. One raised his glass towards Bill in recognition and nodded his head. Bill smiled and gave a wave of acknowledgement back. A formally dressed man greeted us. "Good afternoon gentlemen. Welcome to the To Kalon Club. Doctor McCaw your table is ready in the dining room whenever you are ready." Bill thanked him and proceeded to introduce me to the gentleman as his guest, Doctor Henry Jones. We shook hands.

"I hope you enjoy the club Doctor Jones. Should you wish to join, I can assist you with a membership application." I thanked him, and we parted with Bill leading the way to the dining room. At the dining room door another man greeted us. And escorted us to a table. The table was formally set with silver utensils and crystal glassware. A small card rested on the linen napkin with several choices of meals listed. I ordered the roasted chicken with roasted vegetables, Bill selected pork chops, with garlic potatoes and a garden salad.

We discussed over dinner that Bill would meet me at the morning train for our trip to Howard and he would work with me until noon to get me accustomed to my new assignment. He told me that the General was insistent that he be involved in getting me trained in working in the prison environment. That I would understand the pitfalls that would befall me in dealing with the criminal element. Also, that the staff would feel more confident by seeing a familiar face training the new doctor. Not to mention the prisoners would be more trusting in me knowing that their current doctor was showing me the ropes. Following a delicious dinner we retired to the large lounge for brandy, where Bill introduced me to a number of gentlemen that belonged to the club. We left for Providence about 6:00 o'clock.

We had a very enjoyable afternoon, and actually, it was very informative. We had lengthy discussions about the boss, and how it would be working with him. Bill was very frank about the General's personality. Bill had a good working relationship with the Boss. He had a great deal of respect for him and the life he had led. He was a strict man, but was fair with his dealing with the men in his command and the prisoners under his charge. It was evident, to Bill, that he had a big heart. He told me that much of his tenderness was influenced by his wife, Mary. I climbed the stairs and entered my apartment. Putting the pot on for some tea, I planned to sit and relax for the evening and think about the discussion I had with Bill.

Sunday morning came quickly. I must have been tired, I slept like a baby. I laughed out loud, that expression is silly, babies don't sleep. I put the pot on for tea and started getting ready for the day. Today I will be heading to church. I try to get to church every Sunday. I had promised my mother that I would do that, and I have kept my promise since I arrived in America. Today being Easter, I especially look forward to attending services. I discovered a wonderful church my first week in Providence. Grace Episcopal Church at 300 Westminster Street, is a gothic design and is absolutely beautiful with magnificent stained glass window. The organ pipes must rise twenty five feet into the air. The parishioners are friendly and the Pastor is inspiring with his sermons.

The water is boiling. As I pour my tea a knock came at the door, it was the landlady. "Good morning and Happy Easter Doctor, I made a batch of scones this morning. I thought you would like one with your tea." I thanked her. "I wanted to let you know that I was contacted by an assistant professor at Brown, and he is interested in renting your apartment. I would like to show it to him tomorrow, if that would be convenient?" I assured her it would be fine and that I would not be home, so she could just let herself in. "Do you know when you would be leaving, Doctor?" I told her that this Friday would be my last day here. "That is fine. If the gentleman wants to rent the apartment, I will tell him it will be available on May 1st. That will give me time to ready it for the new tenant. Burt always helps out with some painting and a good cleaning." I offered to pay the full April rent. She thanked me saying she was great full to me not to lose the full months income.

I was off to church. I felt that I was very blessed with everything that had taken place lately. It was time to give thanks to God for his blessings. The church was beautifully decorated for the holiday. The altar area was full of spring flowers, lilies, tulips and daffodils. This afternoon I will write a letter to my mother and father to tell them what a wonderful Easter this year brought me. I have so much to tell them of my adventures in America so far, and will give them my new address.

CHAPTER 4

Howard

The week with Bill has gone well. Monday was a day of nervousness, being the first day I was actually inside the prison with contact with the prisoners. By noon when Bill was leaving I was a little more comfortable. The prison staff was a little standoffish. Much more formal with me than with Doctor McCaw. I shared my concerns with Bill. He assured me that they would come around. "It just seems to be a condition of people working in prison and the jail, it's an us and them type of thinking. In time you will gain their trust and be looked upon as part of the team." The prisoners appeared to be more welcoming than the guards. I was not expecting that to be the case. Bill explained, that. "The prisoners recognize that you are the new guy, and being a doctor you are there to take care of them and their wellbeing. But you are also the new fish in their pond. They will early on try to use the standoffishness of the guards to place a wedge between you and the other staff. They will tell you how unfair they are and how the prisoners are abused by them. They will offer to take care of you, so no one bothers you to make you feel safer with them than the regular staff." I assured Bill that I would be on guard for that. And thanked him for his insight and experience. He told me that I should go and meet with the General tomorrow morning, before I start my first day working on my own. He always wants to sit down and talk individually with every new staff member. Bill had told me at dinner on Saturday how the General wants to get to know every member of the staff of the prison and jail. He puts great store instilling trust in them and they know that they can count on him to be there for them.

I had brought the last of my belonging to my residence at the institutions. The only items I had in Providence was the clothes that I intended to wear on Friday. I told the landlady that I would be leaving on the first train in the morning for Cranston, and that I would leave the key on the desk. She told me that I was welcome to visit her anytime and that I was one of her best tenants that she had ever had. I thanked her and told her to give my best wishes to Burt.

I rose early, put the pot on for my last cup of tea here on Friendship Street. Even though I had started working in the prison on Monday, today would be the first day I will be working alone. Bill will be covering the Alms House and other assignments. He did assure me that he would be available if I needed him, which made me feel a little better. Time to go. I don't want to miss the first train out, and be late my first day alone. I grabbed my doctor's bag, and valise with the last of my clothes, also put the apartment key on the desk and off I went to the train station. It was a chilly morning. We had an overnight snow fall. About two inches that's not unusual for spring in Rhode Island. By noon it will be gone.

While standing on the platform, I looked around at the other passengers, some bound for New Haven Connecticut and New York City. Others, like myself were going to work at the institutions at Howard.

On the far end of the platform were others who were not very joyous in appearance. A motley group of people under guard, heading to the grim castle of despair, a place of sorrow. Everyone boarded the train, the last aboard were those under guard. I watched intently the prisoners as we pulled into the depot. Many of them looked through the car windows to what appeared to be a stately castle of grey stone, a large structure with oval windows, and massive walls with a central dome.

The train slowed and the conductor called out, "Howard Depot!" several times. The train stopped in a cloud of steam and smoke. The sheriffs in their blue uniforms, ushered their prisoners out of the car and onto the wet snowy platform. Calls from the sheriffs brought the motley group to some semblance of order.

The female prisoners were grouped separately from their male counterparts. A uniformed matron took charge of them. One of the females clanking her handcuffed wrists was screaming out some unintelligible words seeming to be insane. One of the other female prisoners was speaking to her with sympathy and a comforting touch to her arm. That touch of tenderness and a smile, calmed the disruptive women, so the officer could attend to the separating shouts of the sheriff about, Asylum, House of Corrections. The sheriff was linked to his prisoners, and splashed through the slush covered walkway towards the Prison and Providence County Jail. The officer with his other prisoners and the shouting insane women climbed the hill to the Asylum for the insane. There he left the women and continued on with the other prisoners to the House of Corrections and State Farm. My thoughts drifted to the flag of the State of Rhode Island, flying at these institutions. A banner emblazoned with an anchor and state motto of "HOPE". For many of those who arrived with me today at Howard Depot there is little hope only despair, fear and sorrow. Hope was a thing of the past.

I walked through the slush up the hill behind the officer and his charges to the residents' hall. There I dropped off my valise, I would unpack it later. I had to make my way over to the Prison. This is the first day that I will be alone without Bill's guidance. Before I make my way to the prison infirmary in the yard. I have to meet with the Boss. Bill had told me it was somewhat of a tradition that the General meets with every new person working in the prison and jail. When I was told about this, I thought what a good idea. I thought it would be a good thing if every boss would sit down with each new employee in whatever business it was. As I walked pasted the fields on my way to the prison, the "honey wagon" was spreading its contents across the un-farrowed ground. The Warden's farm was a tribute to his order and discipline in all he oversaw. His farm was weed less and fruitful. He went by the old proverb that "If you tickled the earth with a hoe it would smile at you with a harvest." The Warden believed in the old Chinese method of "night soil" fertilization. The lack of plumbing in the cells provided an endless supply of fertilizer for the fields.

I arrived at the front of the prison about 8:15, and checked with the officer at the front gate if the Warden was in his office yet. He informed me that the General had just went to his office after checking the perimeter of the facility. He has a routine of riding his buggy around the wall surrounding the prison and jail twice daily, first thing in the morning and just before sunset in the afternoon. I entered the gate and climbed the iron staircase to the Warden's Office.

As I was about to knock on the large wooden door, it opened, and it was Mary the boss's wife. I startled her, as we were face to face at the doorway. "Oh my goodness!" I gave my apologies for scarring her. "Not to worry doctor, I was just bringing Nelson a pot of tea and a couple of biscuits, I thought would be nice to have for your meeting this morning." I thanked her. "I usually bring Nelson a pot of coffee after his rounds. But, I though tea would be better this morning with you being English and all." I smiled and thanked her again for her thoughtfulness. From behind her, I heard her husband call out for me to come in. "I'll be leaving now. The two of you have a lot of things to talk about. I do hope you will be able to join Nelson and me for dinner on Sunday. It is somewhat of a tradition with the new men arriving here you know." I thanked her and told her that it was kind of her to invite me, and that I would be delighted to come to dinner this Sunday. I asked if there was anything I could bring. "No doctor just your fine self would be wonderful, and if there is a Mrs. Jones of course." I told her that I was not married and it is just myself. I looked over Mrs. Viall's shoulder and saw the General patiently waiting for me standing at his desk. "I will see you on Sunday doctor about 1:00pm will be fine." She stepped around me and turned to the right to the doorway leading to the hallway that crossed over the bridge between the prison building and the warden's house.

"Come in Doctor Jones, have a seat. Thank you for joining me today. And how has your week been so far?" I told him that the week has gone well and Doctor McCaw has been very helpful in getting me acquainted with everything in the infirmary. I informed the Warden that I was impressed with the cleanliness and conditions in the infirmary, and that it was a credit to him and the staff. "Thank you doctor. If there is anything that you need or any problems you know that you can always come to me. My door is always open to you. You are a valuable addition to the staff here. I have been trying for some time to have a full time doctor assigned to the prison. Doctor Keene has been a big help and supported my request to the Board." I thanked him for his kind words. "As you have probably noticed, working in a prison can be a challenge and at times it can be a little intimating environment. Many of the prisoners are violent individuals, whose lives have delivered them to my charge. You can rest assured that I have a very competent staff that are always on the lookout for potential problems. Should you have any conflict with any prisoner, you can go to any of them for assistance. Not that I would expect any, but should you have a problem or complaint about any of my staff, you can always come to me for a resolution." Again, I thanked him, and told him what I had told Bill about the feeling I had that the staff was standoffish towards me, and that Doctor McCaw had assured me that that would pass. "Every new person goes through that. He came to me with the same observation when he first started here part time, it didn't take long and he fit right in, as I am sure you will. Just give it a little time." With the pause in the conversation, the Boss poured me and himself a cup of tea. We both enjoyed the biscuits that

Mrs. Viall had provided. "I normally enjoy a strong cup of coffee at this time. Tea is a nice change today." I smiled and told him that his wife had told me we were having tea because I am British and she was kind enough to serve tea in my honor.

"Fine women, Mary. She is an angel God sent to keep me in line. She has a great deal of patience with me. Some people think I can be a difficult man to deal with." We both laughed out loud.

"Doctor, on a serious note, I do want to make it clear to you how important it is to maintain discipline within a jail and prison. I do not allow staff to abuse any of the prisoners, I also do not allow any prisoners to assault or abuse my staff. I do expect the staff to enforce the rules that I gave you a couple of weeks ago, and my staff are expected to defend themselves. I expect that you will ensure that prisoners will show you proper respect as their doctor. Some inmates will allow you to witness a small rule violation, in order to see what you will do. This happens to all new people on the job. How you react to that will go a long way in establishing yourself with both prisoners and staff. You, being the doctor here, no one expects you to act as their overseer. However you need to inform the prisoner that he is breaking a rule and if it continues you will be reporting it to the officer. If you take that approach you will gain the respect of both the prisoners and the staff." I told the Warden that Bill and I had talked about such things and the tests that some prisoners would try with me being the new man. "Good. Early on, Doctor McCaw had a problem he had to come to me with. An inmate tried to befriend him in order to have the doctor bring him something into the prison. Fortunately he went to the Captain about it and the problem was rectified quickly." I told the Boss that Bill had told me about it, and things were fine after that incident. I assured him that I would be on my guard not to be taken advantage of.

"Is there anything that you have seen so far that you have any questions about, or something I may be able to help you with?" I did have something on my mind. I was concerned with the straw mattresses on the beds in the hospital ward. They are not easily cleaned, and being so high on the iron beds, the prisoners could fall to the floor and be injured. But, I decided that this was not the time to confront the General about this, I would bring it up at a later time. After all this is my first official day and I didn't want to give a bad impression or seem to be a trouble maker. I told him that I had nothing pressing to bring up and if I did I knew that I could bring it to him anytime. "Good. One thing to keep in mind doctor. We have a saying in prison. "What happens in prison stays in prison." You can come to me, and I will settle whatever it is. You may, or may not agree with my decision, but it's my decision to make and I will standby that decision. I don't change my mind often once I have decided something." I told the General that I understood, and complimented him on his consistency, and that I was sure that the staff, and prisoners alike, appreciate knowing that he will stay the course. "Doctor I learned a long time ago during the Mexican War, about consistent leadership. Unfortunately for a short time, when I was a Sargent, I had a commanding officer who would make decisions and then in the middle of the action would change his orders. If things didn't go well he would blame his subordinates for the fiasco. I swore that if ever I were to be in command, I would be consistent in my actions and treat my men fairly and be resolute in my leadership. That decision has served me well in my second war and in civilian life."

The boss rose from his desk and that was my signal that our meeting was over and I was being dismissed. "Well, doctor it seems that all is going well. I have spoken to my key staff and they are pleased with how you are doing. That will go a long way in your adjustment to working within the walls." I thanked him again for his support on my appointment. "So, my wife and I will have the pleasure of your company this Sunday for dinner? We will be having chicken. We always have chicken on Sunday." A little smile came to the Boss's lips. Then we both started laughing. "Consistency is a good thing doctor even for your stomach." I told him that I was looking forward to Sunday dinner. We shook hands and I left the Warden's office on a high note. I thought our meeting went extremely well and was sure I had his confidence, and I know he has mine.

On Sunday morning I attended church services at the Chapel at the Training School, a beautiful stone church with a slate roof and belfry. The inside had high ceilings with exposed beams and a large cast iron chandelier lit with candles. It was raised and lowered by a rope pulley that was secured to the far wall. The children confined to the training school were required to attend church each week. The boys and girls attended at different times. There were a number of staff that also attended. I was pleased to see that as it was a positive example to the children.

About 12:30 I began my walk to the Warden's house, arriving about 12:50. Walking up to the front door, I knocked. In a minute or so the door opened and I was greeted by the General. "Come in, doctor, and welcome. How was your morning?" I told him it was a beautiful Sunday morning and I had attended church services at the Training School Chapel. That brought a slight smile to his lips. "Mary and I always attend services here at the prison chapel. I feel it does the prisoners well to see that their Warden and his wife stand before God alongside of them. Join me in the parlor doctor, Mary is just finishing preparing dinner." He took his pocket watch from his vest pocket, and looking at it. "Dinner will be just a few minutes away."

We both took seats in a small but well-furnished parlor. "Doctor Jones, I always enjoy having new staff to Sunday dinner. I gives both of us a chance to get to know each other in an informal setting. May I call you

Henry, Doctor?" I assured him that that would be fine. I asked, "and you sir, what would you prefer? He again smiled and said. "I am called by many names, Henry. The staff usually calls me Boss. Some call me Warden, many other people call me General. Here in my home, feel free to just call me Nelson if you are comfortable with that." With that out of the way, Mrs. Viall entered the parlor. She announced that dinner was ready in the dining room.

We both stood and followed her into the other room. Again the dining room was small but well furnished. The dinner table appeared to be oak and could easily seat six. Against the wall was a china closet containing a beautiful china set, the table was set with a white linen table cloth, and matching napkins. The plates were from the set displayed in the china closet. Each setting had silver knife, fork and spoon on the napkin by the plate. I complimented her on a beautiful table. She seemed to blush slightly and thanked me for being so kind. In the center of the table was a platter of roasted chicken, a bowl of mashed potatoes, along with other bowls containing beets, carrots, and one with what appeared to be bread stuffing. A basket of rolls and butter dish finished off the table. The Boss pulled his wife's chair out for her to take her seat. I waited until the Boss sat to take my place at the table. Mrs. Viall asked her husband to say grace. Mrs. Viall told me to help myself to the food. Saying that the dinner was not a formal occasion, just a getting to know you, and welcoming dinner for me.

"Thank you, Mrs. Viall." She came back with telling me to call her Mary and asked if she could call me Henry. "Oh, of course, please do, call me Henry." Mary passed the platter of chicken to me, taking a piece, I handed the platter to Nelson. Bowls were passed until all had our plates were full of food. "Thank you for inviting me today. This is very unexpected. It isn't often that a person is invited to his boss's home for dinner." Mary told me that this has been somewhat of a tradition of Nelson and herself with all new employees at the prison. She said that she actually looks forward to doing it. She mentioned that with just her and Nelson, it is nice to have company to dinner. Our conversation continued. I was asked about growing up in England and my family. "You and Nelson have children?" I felt the tone change, and Mary told me that they had four children, 2 boys and 2 girls, all of whom had died, two passed away in their first year. Mary passed away at 4 years old and Arthur at age eight while Nelson was away at war. I expressed my condolences on their loss. My doctor's curiosity was piqued but I did not want to cause them any additional pain, so I changed the subject.

Following dinner, Mary served Nelson and I desert and coffee it the parlor, a tasty piece of peach pie. I told Mary that I hadn't had peach pie since my mother's, when I was a boy. She asked how hers measured up, to my mother's. I laughed out loud. "Mary, I must tell you, my mother was not much of a cook. She could burn water. But my father always was complimentary to her on the meals she made. I think it was because he knew that she would tell him to cook for himself if he thought he could do better." We all laughed. "You know the English are not known for their culinary skills."

The conversation was light. I asked Nelson if he would tell me about himself and his experiences. Mary injected, with a smile, that she was going to go and clean up the dishes, that she had heard it all before, and Nelson always enjoyed telling about his life experiences.

The Boss went to the cabinet against the wall and took out two glasses, pouring about two fingers of brandy in both. He handed me my glass and sat back in his over-stuffed chair, taking a sip. "Well, Henry, I wasn't born here in Rhode Island. I was born in Plainfield, Connecticut. My father and mother had more children than money, so at about eleven years old, was sent to live and work for another family, on a farm. I didn't go to college. School was not tops on my list of things to do. When I was about nineteen, I moved to Providence and went to work as a molder in the foundry. I loved learning about the military, and attached myself to the, United Train of Artillery. The war with Mexico was going on and I thought I would join a unit forming in Rhode Island under Captain Pitman. Because of my experience with the Artillery, I enlisted as a corporal, and later was promoted to sargent. I took part in several successful battles in Mexico and after the fall of Mexico City, I stayed for a short time as part of the garrison in Mexico, and came home to Providence." He took another sip of his brandy, and by his eyes I could tell his mind for a short moment was in Mexico. "I went back to the foundry, but I guess I needed more adventure. In fifty, I traveled to Brazil and contracted to build and manage an iron foundry. I came back to Rhode Island in fifty four and went back to the foundry in Providence as a foreman. I remained in the militia as an officer in the Providence Artillery, and when the Civil War broke out, I mustered out as a 1st Lieutenant with the Rhode Island Volunteer Infantry. I was made a Captain of Company D in the 2nd Rhode Island Volunteer Infantry."

Again he took a drink and glanced over to see if he was boring me with his memories. On the contrary, I was waiting for him to continue. "At the first battle of Bull Run, in Manassas, Virginia, things went badly. The rebels kicked our asses. We lost Major Ballou and Colonel Slocum in the battle. I wound up having to assume command and was promoted to Major, then to Lieutenant Colonel. By the battle of Fredericksburg we were up against Lee's army of Northern Virginia. General Burnside had us trying to dislodge the rebels who were entrenched on high ground behind the city. I received a promotion to full Colonel when Colonel Wheaton was made a Brigadier General."

Nelson stood up and walked to the liquor cabinet

and poured himself another glass. He turned to me. "Ready for another, Henry?" I told him I was fine. My glass was still half full, I was so into his recount of his war experiences. "Well, that didn't last long. After I became Colonel, word came down from Rhode Island that a man who was an absolute disgrace was to be promoted to Major, because of his connections back in Rhode Island. He was promoted over my objections so in sixty three, I resigned my commission and went home. I know, it's like I'm going to take my marbles and go home. I was always a bull headed guy. Even as a kid I didn't work and play well with others." We both broke out into laughter. I choked a little on my brandy.

"Had enough yet, Henry?" I told him no please continue, he had me on the edge of my seat wondering how he got to be a General. "When I returned home, I was approached and asked to take command of a new "colored" unit, the 14th Rhode Island Colored Heavy Artillery and was commissioned as a Lieutenant Colonel. I know that this was meant as part of a payback for opposing the promotion of that man as Major. The powers about had no faith in the black soldiers to be a real fighting force. I would up recruiting and training the soldiers of the regiment. We became the 11th United States Colored Heavy Artillery. I served with them in Louisiana around New Orleans, until the end of the war, I was made brevetted Brigadier General, US Volunteers in' sixty-five for my service in the war."

I think Mary was listening from the other room

and thought it was a good time to join us. She asked if I would like some tea and another piece of peach pie. I thanked her and said that would be nice, and finished the last of my brandy. She returned with a tray with my pie and a cup of tea for both of us. She told her husband to please continue, she thought that I was enjoying the Boss's memories. I was actually enjoying myself and learning a great deal how he became the man that he was. Also, American History. "When I returned home, I had become somewhat of a celebrity. I had served with a number of notable Rhode Island men during the war. My commander at Bull Run became a politician and Governor in' sixty-six. The Slocum and Ballou families were both prominent families. Letters home had praised my abilities and leadership in combat.

I tried my hand at politics and got myself elected to the Rhode Island House of Representatives and served one term. That didn't go to well. I never was good at compromising and going along to get a long." He smiled at me over his drink. "In' sixty-seven I was appointed the first Chief of Police in Providence and selected and trained the new force. Training was one of my strong points. You know, Henry one of those Boss things." Another smile. "Governor Burnside in' sixty-seven appointed me Warden of the State Prison and Providence County Jail. Back then it was in Providence along the Providence River. The place was a dump, a terrible place to work and God awful for inmates to live. It was decided to build the facility here in

Cranston and in seventy eight I marched the inmates here from Providence. So, Henry, here we are today, in ninety three, sixteen years later. Still Warden, having dinner with my new full time Physician."

I stood up and walked over to him and shook his hand. I thanked him for sharing his life story with me. Also for his service to his State and Country. After some small talk with Mary and Nelson, I thanked them for a wonderful meal and afternoon. It was already after 5:00pm and I didn't want to monopolize their whole afternoon and evening. I told the Boss that I would be in in the morning and thanked him and Mary again for a wonderful day.

HOWARD TRAIN DEPOT

CHAPTER 5
MEETING OF THE MINDS

I cannot believe how men can live like this. The jail is so crowded some cells made for two men are housing five. The prison is in better condition. Only occasionally being over capacity. I have gone to the General about my concerns that the conditions are ripe for an epidemic, we have been lucky that the prisoners have been spared. He has asked that I meet with him this afternoon to discuss the matter. I am looking forward to sitting down and sharing my concerns. Doctor McCaw gave me a brief history of the problem and told me that Doctor Keene and the Board have been requesting a new jail be built or an addition to the existing one.

I climb the stairs to the Warden's office carrying my notes on the conditions that exists to support my concerns. I knocked on the heavy door. "Come in Doctor." The Boss was behind his desk in his shirtsleeves, his jacket hanging in the corner. This was unusual for him. Whenever he met with someone, he was always in jacket and tie. I thought that this may be a signal that this meeting was to be less formal and more open than I was expecting. The Boss stood and shook my hand as he walked around the desk to greet me. He took a hold of the chair in front of his desk and moved it to the side of his desk, turned slightly towards his chair.

"Doctor, feel free to remove your jacket and take a seat. It is a warm day and we will most likely be here for a while." I did as suggested, hanging my jacket next to his. A smile crossed my face as I noticed how small my jacket was compared to his. We both took our seats. As we did, there was a quiet knock on the door. "Come in."

The door opened and there was the Boss's wife holding a tray with a pitcher of what appeared to be lemonade and two tall glasses. We stood as Mary entered the office. She greeted me and told us she thought we may enjoy a cool drink on a warm early May afternoon.

"Thank you, my dear." The Warden said, I also expressed my gratitude, as she placed the tray on a small side table in the office, and left closing the door behind her. "I am a fortunate man, Doctor." I agreed that he indeed was to have such a considerate wife.

"Now, Doctor. I know from our talk in the infirmary that you are concerned about the conditions in the jail. I have the same concerns as you do. Unfortunately we both have little control over the numbers of prisoners we are sent. The jail holds not only prisoners that are awaiting their trial, we also hold those unable to pay fines and debtors who owe companies. I have been able to have a number of friendly Judges reduce some fines or in place of a fine, have the man do some type of service in the county."

I told the Warden that I understand that he is trying to manage the population as best he can, but I would feel negligent of my responsibilities not to raise my concerns directly to him. Also, I did not want to express these concerns to Doctor Keene and the Board without speaking to him.

"Thank you, Doctor. You know that both the Board of Charities and Corrections along with Doctor Keene have been requesting an expansion of the jail for some years now."

I told him that Doctor McCaw had briefed me about the efforts that have been made.

He stood up and went and poured himself and me a glass of lemonade, and placed it on his desk in front of me. "One of the things that has helped was the fact that a new well has been created and has come on line, providing additional clean drinking water. As you know Doctor, I have ordered additional cleaning in the housing units, and other sanitary measures in hopes to ward off diseases."

I know, Sir and we all appreciate your efforts, including the prisoners. "We have also improved ventilation by bring on line unused steam pipes. We are also doing the same in the prison side of the facility. Are you aware, Henry, that the Legislature had approved and budgeted for a new jail last year?" Actually I had heard that, I said. "Well they pulled the funding and canceled it at the last minute. I took that personal, and I think it might have been. I got into a pissing contest with the chairman of the house finance committee. I have the ear of the Governor Brown. And the chairman wanted to flex his muscles. I think that this was payback. I have been fortunate that during my time as Warden, we have had an almost continuous string of Republican Governors." During my time in the State I have seen what politics is like in Rhode Island, and things can get personal.

"I do have some good news for you, Doctor." The General unrolled a large set of plans across his desk. "Henry, the Board has been able to scrape up enough money from other projects at the institutions and came up with enough funds to construct a wooden housing unit to be built in the yard of the jail. It will be an open barracks type of housing. Construction will start by the end of the month. This is hoped to be just a temporary bandage on the problem, and we will need to be very selective on who we select to be housed in this new building." I told the Boss that if he needed any input from me, I would be happy to assist.

"Thank you, Doctor. We will want to insure that those selected to live in the new housing are healthy. It will be close living quarters. Better than five to a cell but still cramped quarters. It is my intention to loan a number of these prisoners out to do some farm work to local farms. I like to have the prisoners who are here for fines or debts that they are unable to pay work for local farmers that needs help with planting or harvesting. The farmers pay the institution an amount for each prisoner we provide I then apply part of that to their fine or debt. This works well for everyone. The prisoners get paid out of custody, we get an empty bed. It took some convincing to get the Board to agree to the idea. But with the support of Doctors Keene and McCaw, they agreed. As long as it was only those types of prisoners.

I do have the sentenced prisoners working on manufacturing items for private companies, like shoes and shirts. These funds helps to defray some of the operating expenses for the Prison." I told the Boss that, I thought that within reason it was good for the prisoner's mental health to keep them busy. I asked if they received anything for their work. "I found that giving the prisoners a small amount in piece work based on their production was a good incentive. We hold the money they make in a store account and they can spend it here at the facility for smokes and treats."

"Warden, I want to tell you about a meeting I had with Doctor Keene last week. There is a plan to vaccinate all the residents in all the institutions against small pox. I will be examining all our present prisoners to see if they have been vaccinated. Those who have not will be given vaccinations for the disease. We are concerned that we could have an outbreak with the living conditions and that many of our residents are poor and have very little medical care. I will also be offering the staff the opportunity to receive an inoculation if they desire. I know we cannot require them to participate but I intend to make it available."

The General smiled, and told me that any of the staff who have not been vaccinated will participate. "Thank you for your support General." He told me that he had witnessed what a disease like small pox can do to a unit. He experienced an outbreak in Mexico and in Brazil in the short time he was there. "Once I have identified the men needing to be vaccinated, Doctor Keene will be assigning Dr. McCaw to assist in accomplishing the task."

The Warden shared his pleasure with the project and that Doctor McCaw is the perfect person to help out. He is well known to the staff and inmates. He asked for a few days' notice before we would begin, so he could schedule work around the project. "We will also need to check each man in a couple of weeks to make sure the vaccination took."

The Boss made it clear there would be no problem and I had his full support. The last thing he needed was a small pox outbreak. Without me asking or mentioning whether he had been vaccinated he unbuttoned his shirt pulled out his arm to show me that he, indeed had been vaccinated. "Warden there is no need to show me." He explained that this was his way to "encourage" his staff to participate, without twisting their arms. We both laughed.

He picked up his glass and drained the last of the lemonade and stood walking over to the table that held the tray and pitcher. With his back still turned away from me he said. "Henry, I know that I can appear to be a hard man. And I can be that. However I do always have the wellbeing of my staff and those placed under my command here at the facility in mind in the decisions I have to make." He still had his back to me, though he was done placing the glass in the tray. "Henry, I know you also hold concerns for those you care for. There may be times you come to me with your concerns and we may not agree on how to address those concerns. But understand, being in charge of a command such as this, there are many things that weigh upon me and the decisions I have to make. I hope that in times when I have to deny your requests or disagree with you, it is never personal. I value your work and your opinion."

I sat silent, as he walked, still with his back towards me, to his suit jacket. He put it on and turned towards me. I stood and walked for my jacket. I understood the meeting was over. I put my jacket on. "Thank you Doctor Jones, for everything you do." As I shook his hand, I squeezed it a little tighter than I normally did.

And assured him that I understood what he had to say and thanked him for his confidence in me. I left the

Boss's office with a greater understanding of the man I was working for. I felt privileged that he had shared his humanity with me. I am sure that his doing so was not easy for him. And, required him to have a great deal of trust in me not to discuss the vulnerability he showed outside of the office.

Sunday May 14, I decided to attend church services at the Prison Chapel. Reverend Nutting had arraigned for the women's choir from Grace Church in Providence to come to the prison and sing for the services that week. I always enjoyed their music when I lived in Providence.

I climbed the iron stairs to the chapel the prisoners were already seated with guards stationed at each end of the raised stage and one at each of the two door to the chapel. I was directed to the front row of chairs by the Officer in charge, and sat down. Reverend Nutting moved to the podium and told those in attendance that the Women's Choir from Grace Church, would be joining us, and providing the music. Just at that time I heard the door behind us open and the Officer in charge called out "Attention!" All of the prisoners and guards stood at attention. The Chapel was silent.

In walked the Warden and his wife. They joined me in the front row. The Warden was not in his regular jacket and tie. He was sporting his Military uniform to include his sword and red sash indicating that he was an artillery officer. He carried his military hat in his left hand. Mary took her seat next to me and the Warden turned to those present and returned a hand salute to his staff who were saluting him. "Please everyone take your seats."

He turned towards the Reverend. "I'm sorry Reverend for being late. Please continue." And the Warden took his seat with his wife Mary between us.

Reverend Nutting opened his remarks by informing everyone that this was a special day in the State of Rhode Island. He explained that today was "Decoration Day". That it was the day that the State had set aside to remember those who had lost their lives to save this great union during the War Between the States. He said a number of states have also set aside a day in May to commemorate the same event. He took a moment and recognized two of the guards present for their service.

Then, he spoke about General Viall and his service in the war. Without encouragement all the prisoners and staff present rose to their feet in applause. The Boss was a little embarrassed and thanked everyone and asked them to be seated.

The Reverend continued telling everyone that the General and his wife would be spending the rest of the day in various cemeteries in the state placing flowers at the graves of those who fell in battle. The flower were grown here on the prison farm and have been gathered by some of your fellow prisoners. So, in a way, the Warden will be representing you today in recognizing those who lost their lives in service to the State and the Nation. Again applause broke out. The choir broke out in singing the "Battle Hymn of the Republic". Several other hymns were song by the choir and Scripture readings.

The Reverend delivered a wonderful homily. At the end of the service the Reverend thanked the Women's Choir for coming and sharing their beautiful voices with us. Again applause from those in attendance. The Warden and his wife went up onto the stage to thank the choir personally, as the guards cleared the Chapel of the prisoners. I joined them and also thanked the Reverend Nutting for his sermon, and the choir. I also greeted Mary telling her she looked wonderful. She blushed slightly. I went to the General. "A fine figure of a man you are in your uniform, Sir." He shook my hand and pulled me in close to him and said in my ear that Mary had to let it out a little. We both started laughing, as Mary looked wondering what the Warden had said to me that was so funny.

I asked the General if he would like me to go with him and Mary to help place the flowers. I had no plans for the day. "Thank you, Doctor, for offering. But, this is something I want to do alone. Kind of a "Final Good Bye" to those I served with and gave their lives under my command."

CHAPTER 6
My PRACTICE

I soon discovered being a prison doctor came with many duties and experiences. I found that I would gain more experience as a doctor in three months working in the prison than three years in private practice. I treated a number of conditions that I may have never come across in any other setting or in a private practice.

Bill McCaw had steered me in the right direction, before I started, and his assistance over the past few months have been essential in gaining the experience I needed to be an effective doctor in the facility. With Bill's assistance we completed the vaccination of all jail and prison inmates for small pox. Thanks to the Boss, we were able to also vaccinate all staff member who had not been vaccinated. He does have a persuasive nature about him. To my surprise, we had one officer, who after receiving three vaccination attempts, his vaccination hadn't taken. Doctor McCaw and I decided that he appeared to have a natural immunity to the pox. Bill had seen this situation before, with a seaman from Portugal he had treated. I recorded our findings in the officer's personal file, to insure that his immunity was on the record. The Warden was also informed so the officer would not have any problems from him.

One of the first inmates I had to place in quarantine a William McCarty, passed away in the hospital from influenza, July 17th. Flu deaths was not uncommon, but he was my first that I had diagnosed. Most of my patients with flu did survive with treatment.

Every day was an adventure. On my way to the infirmary I would always make two stops. The first in the kitchen to make an "Un-official" inspection to ensure cleanliness. The Chief Steward I think looked forward to the visit. He was always happy to show off his kitchen. He often said that the prison kitchen was so clean and well-kept that he would have his family eat here rather than any of the fancy establishments in the city. I never missed a chance to compliment him on his work. I also would stop to walk through the wooden barracks in the yard. With so many jail prisoners living there it was an important visit to make. Both the staff and the inmates felt better after my visit.

They knew well that in such conditions disease could spread rapidly. The guards would give me a heads up on any inmate that they thought maybe was needing to be checked on. Some of the prisoners did not want to come to sick call for fear of losing their job. The little bit of money they made would go to paying their fine or debt. So not working actually lengthened their time in jail.

Upon my arrival at the Infirmary, I would check on any prisoners in the ward. Any who have improved enough to be discharged back into the cell house, names were given to the officer and moved back into the population. At times this was a challenging call. Living in the infirmary was better living conditions. Even with the iron beds and straw mattresses it was better than a cot or the floor of a cell. The Warden was adamant that no prisoners were allowed to malinger in the infirmary. He would on a weekly basis tour the Infirmary to check on the condition of the inmates and the operation. It also gave him the opportunity to visit with me one on one. This I always saw as my opportunity to talk to him about some of the changes I would like to see take place. On occasion I was able to accomplish some improvements. Or plant a thought into the Boss's head, allowing him to come up with a "Progressive policy change".

Today he showed up just in time for the medication line and sick call. I was surprised to see him so early in the day. A change in his routine, for him. Most days he walks the jail and the prison housing first thing in the morning. He took a seat so each inmate had to walk by him as they passed through the line.

Many of the prisoners greeted him with a "Good

Morning, Warden or Sir". The Boss's response was always the same, "Good Morning Charlie". To the Boss everyone was Charlie. It made it easy to remember everyone's name, and it became, somewhat of a laugh to the prisoners. They would get a kick out of the new inmates who would try to correct the Warden with their real name.

The Boss sat in the chair, with a loaded pistol tucked into his belt. The pistol was within easy reach of any of the inmates walking by in the line. Not one would make a move for the weapon. Reading their faces, the thought seems to never cross their minds. As I thought to myself, I think a combination of fear and respect for the man overcame any thought that may have come to them to take the change at snatching the pistol from him.

Abruptly, a guard came into the Infirmary and went up to the Warden telling him something I didn't catch. He stood quickly, "Doctor, get your bag and come with me." We walked quickly out of the Infirmary door, and broke into a jog heading towards the main gate of the prison yard. "Henry, there has been an accident at the barn, we will take my carriage."

As we reached the Iron Gate it opened and closed behind us. Gate two opened before us and we continued to jog to the carriage house. The Warden's horse was already harnessed to the carriage ready for his normal tour around the prison and jail perimeter. We climb up and sat together, "Get up!" the Boss yelled.

His horse responded to its master's voice, his instincts told him of the urgency. We sped down the road, taking the right turn towards the main barn of the prison farm. I thought we were going to roll the carriage over. It righted itself, and we arrived at the barn.

The Boss leapt from his seat just before we came to a halt. I was shocked by how agile he was, at sixty seven years old. He was a good fifty feet ahead of me entering the barn. He plowed through a group of inmates and a guard. He slid onto the ground at the injured officers head. No matter the mixture of manure and straw that littered the floor. A number of the inmates and the guard told me that he had been trying to get an ox to go into his stall and the animal became unruly. The large fifteen hundred pound animal crushed him between the wall and himself. With the Warden cradling his head, I took out my stethoscope and listened to his chest.

The injured officer had his eyes closed, but was conscious. "Anderson, how you doing, man?" The man replied softly to the question from the Warden, that he was having some trouble breathing and his chest felt like the ox was sitting on him.

I opened his uniform and felt his chest. I suspect broken ribs, but his lungs don't appear to have been punctured. "What do you need us to do, doctor?" I told the Boss that we needed to get him to the hospital here at the institutions. We had to move him genially, not to have one of the ribs puncture one of the lungs.

"James, we are going to move you to the wagon. We will try to be gentle, but it will probably hurt a lot." The officer nodded his head.

With the Boss holding his head steady, eight men seven prisoners and the guard lifted him. Four on each side. They carried him to a waiting wagon lying him in the bed. I climbed aboard, the Warden and I road with Officer Anderson to the hospital. When we arrived there were two men in white coats waiting with a stretcher. We helped them get Anderson on it and carried him into the hospital.

Waiting were Doctors McCaw and Latham. Doctor Daniel Latham was a graduate of the Medical School of Maine and was interning at the institutions. I knew him well, he lived in the residence hall where I lived on the first floor. As we were examining the Officer, his wife arrived escorted by Frank Viall. Frank went to the barn and picked up the Boss's carriage and went for Jim's wife.

The Andersons live in one of the houses provided by the State. Being "Barn Boss" Officer Anderson's hours were extensive, five in the morning until three in the afternoon many times later. The couple had four children, three boys and a girl. The Warden was speaking quietly to her as she sobbed. I walked over to them.

"Mrs. Anderson, I'm Doctor Jones. Your husband appears to have several broken ribs. He is in good hands here at the hospital. I know both the doctors who are treating him, and they are very capable men."

The three of us walked to the treatment table where the Officer was lying. The Boss and I stepped aside to give them some privacy. After a few minutes the Warden walked over to the couple. Mrs. Anderson asked the Boss what they were going to do. How would they get by, with Jim being laid up? Would they have to move out of the house?

The Warden and I escorted Mrs. Anderson into a small office near the treatment office. "Georgiana, don't worry everything will be alright. You and the children don't have to move. Jim will be fine. Isn't that right, Doctor?" I assured her that he would be ok. That it may be six to eight weeks before he would be able to work, but he would heal up just fine.

The Warden assured her the family would be receiving Jim's pay as he was injured performing his duties. "Now you don't be worrying about anything, Georgiana. That's what I get paid to do. Everything will be just fine. Now, how about we go see your husband and put his mind at ease. I know him, and I am sure he is more worried about you and the children and who will oversee the barn operation, than himself." The doctors were done with their examination of the Officer and stood to the side of the hall discussing his condition. I joined them while the Warden and Mrs. Anderson went to Jim's side.

"How does he look?" Doctor, McCaw said that it appeared that he had broken two ribs on his left side. But there didn't appear to be any internal injuries.

Doctor. Latham said how lucky he was, that being a large man cushioned him. They indicated that he would need to remain in observation at the hospital a few days to insure that there were no complications. They were going to brace and tape his chest up to protect and stabilize him. "He should be walking around as much as he can to prevent pneumonia from setting in." They agreed but not for a couple of days. They wanted him in bed lying flat to keep the chest stable.

The Warden came over to us. "Shall we go, Doctor? It appears he is in good hands. Mrs. Anderson is staying here for a while. We will get her back to the house to the children when she is ready." Doctors McCaw and Latham assured us they would stay on top of the situation and let us know if there were any complications, but that none were expected.

The Boss and I went outside and climbed into the carriage. We headed down the hill from the hospital. "Doctor, I have a stop to make before we go back to the prison." The Warden drove the carriage back to the barn. Wait here Doctor I will be right back."

An officer and two prisoners met him just outside the barn. I couldn't hear what they were saying, but I assume it involved the operation of the barn and the condition of Officer Anderson. All three walked into the barn. In a few seconds I heard three shots ring out. My heart jumped into my throat.

I looked up as the Boss was walking out of the barn with his pistol still smoking in his hand. He pushed it back into his belt just before climbing back up into the carriage. As he sat in the seat he looked at me. "This Sunday we are having beef for dinner at the prison. That dammed Ox he was always a problem. You can never let things like this happen without consequences." I thought I was glad it was the Ox and not a person that injured Anderson.

As we road back to the facility, the Warden told me he wanted to talk for a while in his house before we went back inside to work. "We need to talk, Doctor. I should have had this talk with you earlier, but I just never got around to it."

We arrived back at the prison. After a ride around the walls of the facility the Boss parked the carriage at the carriage house turning the horse and carriage over to an older black prisoner who was part of the Wardens "House Staff". "How's Mister Anderson, Boss? Said a prayer for him when I heard what happen. He's a good God fearing man, Boss. Always treats me good. Nice family man, he is." The Warden thanked him for his concern, and assured him that he would be alright. He then introduced me to the prisoner. Telling me his name was Charlie. I smiled at the Warden almost laughing.

"Doctor, Sir, my name is really Charlie. Charles Brown the third, Sir from the day I was birthed right here just up the road." I shook his hand with a smile. The Warden and I left and walked to the house.

We went into the Warden's residence and Mrs.

Viall met us. She inquired on the condition of Mr. Anderson. I told her that there didn't appear to be anything life threatening, but he will take some weeks to heal up enough to get back to work. Mary told the Boss that she would go up to the Andersons and check in on Georgiana later to see if she needed anything. The Boss thanked her, and told her to tell Georgiana that we would take care of anything they needed.

"Doctor, I am putting on the pot for tea would you like a cup?" I looked at the Warden and he told me that we would be a while, and feel free to have your tea. "I know, Nelson you will have coffee." I smiled at the Warden, and he smiled back. We were both thinking what a fine woman Mary was.

I followed the Warden into the parlor. His removing his jacket was my clue that this talk would be informal. I removed my jacket and we both took a seat. There was a long pause in conversation and the Boss started with…"Doctor, how do you like your practice here at the Prison?" I told him, it is very challenging, but I do enjoy the work and the experience I am gaining as a young doctor. At first the question took me by surprise, then worried me. I wondered if he was not pleased with my work and was planning to replace me.

"Henry, we didn't have this conversation. I imagine, that Dr. McCaw didn't go into all the duties he assumed here at the Prison. Other than caring for the prisoners and ensuring clean and healthy living conditions. I view the staff and their families as a part of my and Mary's family. I learned early in my military career that a part of leading men was that they feel you care about them. If your troops feel that you care about them and their wellbeing, they will follow you into the most dangerous of situations, without question. Why? Because they trust that you will take care of them, living, dying, and in death. I carry that with me as Warden. Today, what happened to Jim Anderson touched me as if he were my own family. I will take care of him, Georgiana and his kids until he is able to do for himself. He understood that from the moment that fucking ox crushed him." I was beginning to understand where the conversation was going.

"Bill was more than the part time doctor here, he was the doctor for the staff and their families also. The fact he had his private practice made it a little easier. He saw many of the staff and family members at his office in Providence, without charge. I was always able to find a way to compensate him for his extra care he gave." The Boss was right. Bill had never told me the whole story about being doctor for the prison. The words of the Warden only made me admire Doctor McCaw more than I already did. It went a long way in explaining the close relationship that was evident he had with the prison staff.

Mary came into the room with our coffee and tea, and placed the tray on the table, and left the room. The Boss continued. "Doctor, Keene is a fine man, and administrator, so are the members of the Board, however

I never saw the need of informing them of the arrangement Doctor McCaw and I had. We kept it between us. Now you know, I hope that you will keep the agreement I had with Bill between the three of us." I assured him that what he had told me would remain between us.

I knew where the conversation was going. I didn't want to put the Boss in the situation of having to come out and asking me to continue with the arrangement he had with Bill. As the Warden took a sip of his coffee.

I said, "Warden, I would be honored if you would allow me to continue serving our family here at the prison." It was my turn to take sip of my tea, while what I had just said sunk into the Boss's mind. "I don't have a private practice, or office, however, I can make house calls and see staff here at the Prison Infirmary." The Boss smiled over his coffee cup. I knew that my practice had just expanded. The Warden thanked me for my offer. We stood and shook hands, and the deal was sealed. The agreement that had been just struck was never spoken about again. I just became normal business and practice of being the "Prison Doctor".

About a week later, the Warden did give me a small office on the second floor of the prison near his office. He told me it was a better place to see any member of the staff. It was better than the infirmary under the eyes of prisoners or any of the "women visitors", forerunners of the Social Workers who came in on occasion to "do good things" for the poor unfortunate prisoners.

After finishing my day at the prison I returned to the

Residence Hall. Doctor Latham was seated in the parlor sipping a drink. I walked over and inquired how Officer Anderson was doing.

"He is a lucky man. We are keeping him under surveillance and monitoring him with the sphygmomanometer. To make sure his blood pressure is good. We want to make sure that there are no internal injuries or bleeding. Our observations so far are positive. We may release him for home care in two or three days. We want to get him walking around first. It would be helpful, Henry if you could keep an eye on him every once in a while at his home."

I assured him that once he is released from hospital I would keep an eye on him. "I was just going over to the cafeteria for dinner. Would you like to join me, Henry?" I agreed and told him I would go change and meet him here in about fifteen minutes.

HOUSE OF CORRECTIONS FARM

CHAPTER 7
CAST OF CHARACTERS

Officer Anderson was discharged from the hospital and was now back to work at the barn. He did heal faster than I expected. I think one reason he got back to the job so quickly was while he was home recuperating the Superintendent of the State Farm attempted to take over a disputed field that was to the right of the Jail section of the facility. Early one morning while Jim was resting at home, the Superintendent had his charges plow the field reading it for planting.

The Boss assumed that Jim had assigned his crew to ready the field. When the Warden discovered that it was workers from the State Farm, he headed out to find the Superintendent.

I was not present, but the story that was told to me was. The General stormed into the Superintendent's Office, pistol in hand, in front of a number of people he confronted the Superintendent in the hallway outside the office. And declared that he would shoot him if he ever found him on the State Prison premises. There was no doubt in the Superintendent's mind that he meant what he had said. The dispute over that piece of property ended that day.

As time passed, I became fascinated by some of the prisoners and their personalities. We had a prisoner from Connecticut, Dennis Murphy. He was called "Spiker" and was in prison for murder. He was a large and intimidating man. A typical Irishman, loud and outgoing and could talk the ears off a donkey. He worked in the kitchen, a number of long term prisoners was assigned to kitchen duty. The consistency of the staff added to the clean and orderly operation.

The Chief Steward William Towne, recognized that they took ownership and pride in doing a good job when they knew that this was there long term job. Even though the kitchen staff was awaken very early for work, there were advantages to kitchen duty.

He had injured himself and was sent to the Infirmary to be tended to.

"How did you acquire the name Spiker?" I asked while I was treating his burn. He asked why I had asked him about it. "Just curious I guess. I know what you are doing time for and the name can be a little intimidating." He came out with a big laugh. He explained that he had worked for the railroad on maintaining the tracks. He got the nickname of Spiker because that's what his job was. He drove the spikes into the timbers that held the tracks in place. He was in prison because he had killed a man in a bar fight. He was drunk and hit a guy who was making fun of him. The man went down and hit his head on the corner of the bar and died. He told me that it was all an accident, but here he is. He said, "to tell you the truth Doctor, the nickname happens to be a good one for him in prison". Prisoners tend to leave him alone. We both laughed.

There were a large number of prisoners doing time for murder. It may seem strange to those outside the prison, but for the most part, murderers are your best inmates. I found that there were many types of murders. I will attempt to explain. One category, are those who killed a spouse, or another person close to them. They for the most part are remorseful and whatever brought about the act is over and done with. Another category are those who have unintentionally killed someone, like Spiker. Again they also are remorseful.

There are also those who are in the business of killing. These are murders who for a price will kill someone for someone else. There is nothing personal, it makes no difference whether they know the individual or they don't know the person at all, there is no remorse, no feeling, it is just business. Most of the murders I have met in prison fall into these categories. There are a few who kill without reason. They seem to get some type of sick thrill from committing murder. These are the exception to the rule, and because of the randomness of the acts are the most dangerous.

On September 13th of 93 we had a rapist named James Taylor escape from a prison detail. This man is a danger to all women in the community. He has been sentenced for multiple rapes in Rhode Island and Massachusetts and was sentenced to life in prison. It is believed that he is trying to make his way to New York.

The Warden has spoken to several prisoners who he was friends with to gather information. The consensus seems to be that he timed his escape to coincide with the train schedule that goes to New York passed the Howard Depot. He could have jumped aboard as it slowed passing through the depot. There is no doubt in my mind that he will rape again.

The majority of the prisoners are serving time for property crimes, such as breaking and entering, robbery, pick pocketing, or shoplifting. Most the causes, in my opinion, were brought about by social conditions. Being poor, and lack of education and unemployment will lead even the most pious of men to consider committing a crime such as these. If some of these social conditions can be solved, I am sure the population of those poor who are confined here would decrease.

A constant worry is that of suicide. This is a particular problem within the prisoners in the jail. It is not uncommon, I am sorry to say. New prisoners who have never been in jail or prison before, many of whom are young, foster thoughts of taking their own lives. Sitting in his cell, viewing the massive walls that detains him, seeing the representatives of law in uniform, the Warden and Guards. There comes upon the prisoner a mindset dwelling upon how he can escape from his physical and mental captivity. He loses his identity and personality. He is to each day tread the sameness of the institutional routine. Some turn to a plan of physical escape. Others, plan a mental escape, and take their own lives. In my short time working in the prison, I have seen many attempts that prisoners have made to take their lives. Some of which were very strange. The most common, and unfortunately the most successful, is by hanging. Others cut themselves. One man attempted poisoning himself with bleach from the laundry. The most recent successful suicide was September 26th. A prisoner named Moran was found hanging in his cell. This caused me great distress, because I had spoken to him the day before. He had mentioned to me that he had just been sentenced to five years and was depressed that he would have another sentence to do. He had been in prison before and had done a couple of short terms. I assured him that he could do his time, that he knew his way around the prison and had other inmate friends to support him. I dismissed him with little thought of our conversation until I arrived at the prison the next morning and found out what he had done. I feel that he was reaching out to me and I let him down.

Another inmate, Martin Dalton, became a well know prison inmate. He was committed just last year in July for robbing a train. He was sentenced to life for the robbery. An unusually harsh sentence for committing robbery. But powerful owners of the railroad convinced the court that he needed to be made an example of. They were concerned that if he was not given a long sentence, others may try to follow his example and place passengers in danger. And if travelers did not feel safe taking the train it would affect business. He became an instant hero to many of the poor inmates. They viewed him as a guy who dared to strike back at the rich and powerful, a kind of a Robin Hood.

There are a class of prisoners who were labeled as D.D or defective delinquents. These men lived terrible lives in the prison. Men with low intelligences and almost childlike emotions. Their crimes were, for the most part, minor some degenerate in nature. Unlike the alcoholics, who had a thirty or ninety day sentences. These men received indeterminate sentences. Keeping them incarcerated for many years or life. They became forgotten men, lost in the system. Many of them, with the help of the Warden, I was able to get them transferred to one of our mental hospitals or the criminally insane unit. This help ease the crowded conditions. One such inmate was Jimmy. He was a low functioning farm hand who was a sexual deviant. He was sent to prison for having sex with farm animals. His prison life was one of constant harassment from inmates and staff. I feared he was an inmate who was destine to attempt suicide.

The alcoholics, many of whom were regulars, were well known by staff. They would be locked up again and again over the years. Some found that by being locked up for ninety days in the winter season they had a warm bed and three meals a day. Many of them worked on local farms over the spring and summer and would start drinking after the harvest. Being sober in jail they were good inmates and workers who usually were given jobs cleaning the housing units. Some required being kept in the infirmary when they first came into "dry out". They would go through a condition referred to as the "D.T's", Delirium Tremens. They would have periods of hallucinations and become agitated.

One such occasion was sad but comical. The prisoner was in his cell standing on his bed screaming. The guard rushed to the cell to see what the commotion was all about. He asked the man what was wrong. The prisoner was pointing to the corner of the cell telling the guard to get the dog out of the cell. He was frozen with fear. Another officer arrived to the commotion. He told the other officer to open the cell door. When he did, the guard jumped in and began wrestling with the imaginary dog. And dragged it out of the cell and kicked into the air, as if kicking the dog away. The poor inmate climb off the bed, looked around the cell and under the bed. He put his arms around the guard, hugging him and thanking him for getting rid of the dog. A sad example of the evils of alcoholism.

There were a number of homosexuals in the prison.

One of whom was always doing things to get a laugh. On one occasion he was under observation in the infirmary for possible flu. That morning breakfast was hard boiled eggs. During the morning med line, I heard laughter coming from the ward. The officer monitoring the medication line and I went to see what was going on. There in the middle of the ward, the inmate was walking around clucking like a chicken and dropping eggs from his anus that he had placed up inside himself. He was well enough to be discharged from the infirmary. That evening I told one of my colleagues at the resident hall the story about the eggs. I thought he was going to choke, he was laughing so hard. I later thought I shouldn't have told anyone, it could be considered doctor, patient confidentiality.

Another prisoner, Louie, had some mental health issues and needed to be medicated to control his behavior. I had been working on getting him transferred to the Criminally Insane unit. One day he was getting his haircut. He had a habit of carrying his belongings around in a paper sack. He placed them on a table in his view while his hair was being cut. The inmate barber picked up the sack to move it out of his way and Louie went berserk, grabbing the scissors from the inmate barber and stabbing him. The guard subdued him and placed him in a straightjacket, in the black cell, to maintain control of him for several days.

I have been trying to convince the General to stop using the straightjacket on inmates. There have been a number of occasions that its use has caused permanent injury to the men. On another occasion, he attacked a new officer who was passing out bed sheets. The regular guard knew not to touch the new sheets being given to Louie. He would just hold the stack out and Louie would select his sheets from the center of the stack. The new man grabbed the top two sheets and just handed them to him. That's all it took for Louie to go after him.

Some of the staff had some minor oddities in behaviors, nothing that could be considered odd enough to threaten their employment. One officer if you watched him walk, would not step on a crack in the floor. His gate looked almost like a dance as he walked the cell house. Another always repeated the last two words in a sentence twice. An example is, "I will be taking tomorrow off, tomorrow off". Or, "Good morning Doctor, morning Doctor." The prisoners called him, "Mr. Two Times", not to his face of course.

The Warden was not a man who ran the prison from his office. You could call him a hands on administrator. He wasn't a Boss who was afraid to get his hands dirty. On one occasion, a defiant prisoner could not be gotten out of his cell when ordered to do so by the Guards. The situation was reported to the Warden, he walked down to the cell. The plan of the prisoner was to fling the bucket of slops at the guard as soon as he started to open the cell door. The Boss ordered the guards to go to the adjoining cells and fill up a bucket of "slops" and bring it to him. He ordered the guard to open the cell door wide and quickly, and the General covered the prisoner with the contents of the bucket. Before the man could get on the defensive, the General sprang in and flung him out into the corridor, where the Boss initiated various procedures of applied force. Once the prisoner was under the Warden's control the officers took the restrained man to the "black cell" to reflect on his actions. All the way to the cell the prisoner kept apologizing to the Warden. I am sure that Mary was not a happy wife when she heard of the incident. Not the actions of a 66 year old man would be engaged in. At least she didn't have to clean his suit.

This year we had an outbreak of scarlet fever in the most crowded part of the Jail. I had the patient promptly isolated together with three others who occupied the same cell and were exposed. It required the institution be rigidly quarantined and thoroughly disinfected preventing the further spread of the disease. I was always on watch for the breakout of a communicable disease. A situation that the General was most familiar with from his military years. He experienced that disease often killed more troops than the enemies bullets. In the institution, disease prevention was more important that the treatment. The wooden barracks constructed in the yard, I hope will temporarily relieve the dangerously crowded conditions, but it should never be depended upon for a permanent solution for living quarters.

CHAPTER 8
LIFE CHANGING EVENTS

I had dinner with Frank and Alice Viall on Sunday. It was an enjoyable day. As always, whenever men come together talk always seems to revolve around work. After dinner Frank and I went outdoors to enjoy the fall afternoon with a drink and Frank always enjoys a cigar. Alice prefers he not smoke "those smelly things" in the house. Frank told me that Deputy Warden Rowe was planning on moving on. He and his wife were going closer to her family in Connecticut. The position of Deputy Warden would be opening up.

I asked if he knew who would be promoted to the position. Frank informed me that there were a lot of rumors going around. Even that someone may come in from outside the prison system as a political favor to someone. You can never tell what will happen with politics the way it is in the State. I mentioned that the

General would be fit to be tied if political pressure were to take place.

The Deputy's position is an important position in the institution and the person getting the job would need the support of the staff to accomplish the job. It would be hard for an outsider to just come in without experience.

"I think the two inside men comes down to Phil Weaver the Hall Keeper and Ed Slocum the Overseer", Frank told me. "But the official appointment has to come from the Board of Charities and Corrections."

I told him that it was my experience, from my appointment that the General has quite a bit of influence on who is hired for all jobs at the Prison. Frank laughed, "He's a strong personality, and is very popular at the State House. It would take someone with a lot of balls to make an end run around the Boss." I asked, who he thought would be the best choice for Deputy.

He took a sip of his brandy and a few puffs of his cigar. "I think both Phil and Ed are both very capable men, and I like them both. Either of them would be an excellent choice and would be supported by the staff." I pushed a little more, and asked who he thought the General would recommend to the Board? Again a sip of brandy and more smoke from his cigar. I could tell Frank was toying with me. "Knowing Uncle Nelson, and his loyalty to those he served in the war with, my money would be on Ed Slocum. His Dad John was the General's commanding officer and was killed at the first battle of Bull Run. He is very close to the Slocum family and my bet would be on him. If he wants the job, I think he can have it. Even Phil could accept that decision, and back up his promotion." We walked back to the house.

"Henry, I hope you will keep this conversation just between us. I wouldn't want it to get out before it is made public. I haven't spoke to the Boss on what he plans to do, this talk is all just speculation." I told Frank that it was just between us, and how it unfolds will be interesting to watch.

The end of September, Al Rowe announced, to the staff, his decision to leave his position as Deputy Warden at the Prison. That day rumors were flying on who his replacement would be. Some even mentioned that Frank Viall may be named, after all he is the warden's nephew. That was definitely a real long shot. The Chief Clerk's position was key to the orderly business operation of the Jail and Prison. It would be more difficult to replace Frank than just about any member of the staff. Also, not to take anything away from Frank, he was not a leader. He is a good man, a hard worker and a competent business man. But not a man that the staff would feel comfortable following into the fray of battle. Another name that surfaced was Day Officer Millard. He is relatively new to the Prison. He has been there just about a year. But, he is connected to a State Senator by marriage, and has always boasted about his political connections to some members of the staff.

Monday October 2nd, the Warden called a staff

meeting in his office for 4:00pm. I was surprised that I was asked to attend. I didn't view myself as a member of the Command Staff of the facility. Present were Al Rowe the outgoing Deputy Warden, Chief Clerk Frank Viall, Hall Keeper Phil Weaver, Chief Steward Bill Towne, Tom Henry a Senior Day Officer, and Overseer Ed Slocum, and myself. The seven of us sat around a large table awaiting the arrival of the Boss. Little small talk was taking place. We all knew why we were called to the meeting. The Warden was going to announce the new Deputy Warden. The absence of Millard was an obvious indication that the new Deputy Warden appointment was not coming from down town.

Ed and Phil had been the first to arrive and were talking as the rest of us arrived at the room. The presence of Tom Henry was a surprise to me. As myself, I didn't view him as a part of the inner circle Command Staff. The Warden entered the room. As his last official act as Deputy Warden, Al Rowe called the room to attention. As he took his seat at the head of the table, the Boss asked us to be seated.

"Thank you gentlemen for attending. I know you all are very busy. I will try to be brief. I want to take this opportunity to recognize the service of Deputy Rowe. He has been my right hand for some time now and I want to thank him for his faithful service to the Prison, and the State. I will miss his advice and confidence. Al if you could stand, I have a certificate of appreciation from the Governor for your faith full service to the State of Rhode

Island." Everyone joined in a round of applause. "I know that you all wish Al well as he moves on to duties at the Connecticut State Prison. I have assured Warden Washburn that he is gaining an excellent new member to his staff. I have known Warden Washburn for over five years. I know Al and he will work well together." The time had come for the Boss to make the announcement that we have all been waiting for.

"Over the last couple of weeks, I have been discussing with a number of trusted advisors and members of the Board of Charity and Corrections who would make a good replacement for Al Rowe. After interviewing the two leading candidates, I have forwarded to the Superintendent, Doctor Keene, my recommendation. This morning I was contacted by the Superintendent that my recommendation was unanimously approved by the Board."

I thought, Oh come on, General, stop toying with us, and tell us. "I am announcing that the new Deputy Warden for the Jail and Prison will be Overseer Ed Slocum." The room erupted in applause, with pats on the back and handshakes all around the table. "I am sure you will all put your support behind Ed and assist him however you can. He has agreed to accept a very difficult job. After all, he has to deal with me on a daily basis." The room joined in laughter.

I gave my personal congratulations to our new Deputy. Tom Henry was by my side. "Tom, I was as surprised that you are here as much as I was that I was asked to be here." Tom smiled and informed me that he has been with the General ever since he was Chief of Police. The Boss brought him with him when he was made Warden in '68. Being one of the longest serving officers at the prison, the General stays in touch with the line staff, and their concerns, through him. He said how honored he is to have served with a man, such as the Warden, for all these twenty five years.

The holidays are very difficult times in the prison. For the most part the field and farm work has been finished for the year. The fields have been harvested, the hay is in the barn. Prisoners have time on their hands to think of family and their fate being in prison. Only a small crew are working in the barn, caring for the livestock. The late fall the pigs are slaughtered and the smoke house is working.

Thanksgiving was a special holiday for the General. In the fall of 1863 President Lincoln issued a proclamation declaring that the last Thursday in November would be a day of national thanksgiving. The Civil War years were a difficult period in the Warden's life. Being a pious man, he felt it most important to give thanks to God for all the Blessings He has bestowed upon us.

Thanksgiving week each year the Warden allows "a special visit" for all of the inmates with their families. He also releases any inmate that is locked up for violation of the prison rules. A special meal is provided to all the inmates and staff that are on duty that day. All the workshops and work details are shut down with the exception of the caring for the animals. The Boss reduces the staffing to give the men with families the day off staffing the facility with the single officers. Nelson and his wife dine with the inmate population. This year, I joined them at their table, along with Reverend Nutting and Father Coffey. Both clergy deferred giving the prayer of Grace to the Warden.

Following the meal, I was surprised by the grateful applause from the inmate population. Most of those at the dinner had never been served such a bountiful meal in their lives. "General, I have not had such a wonderful meal since we dined on ox." The Warden almost choked with laughter. He stood and called the mess hall to order. He complimented Bill Towne the Chief Steward and his staff for the wonderful meal. And recognized the long hours that went into its preparation. Thanksgiving was a grand day. I must say though that I had my concerns. Ed Slocum had given me a heads up on the tradition that the Boss had in place for Thanksgiving. I did inform Ed of my concern about the short staffing for the day. He assured me that there was not one prisoner who would spoil the day by acting out or attempting to take advantage of the situation by escaping. If he did, the other prisoners would see to it that he would never see Christmas Day.

Winter had set in early and by Christmas we had several inches of snow. It was a cold walk from the Residence Hall to the Prison every morning. It was still dark when I set out. I was careful that the guards in the towers knew it was me coming down the hill behind the prison wall. They would give me a wave of recognition as I passed by on my way to the main entrance. Christmas was a particular difficult time for me. I missed my family back in England. My parents were getting older, and I had thoughts that as time passed I may not see them in person again.

Thanksgiving was the Warden's day, but Christmas was Ed Slocum's day. The Deputy was in charge. The Boss and his wife traveled to Connecticut by train to spend time with Nelson and Mary's family. Christmas was not a grand a celebration as Thanksgiving was. But Ed had a small gift for each staff member. The inmates were each given a small sack of sweets, hard candy, a treat that they rarely had outside of prison, and never inside. I mentioned to Ed how generous he was and that the gifts must have set him back quite a bit. Smiling he whispered into my ear, "Frank is a very creative Clerk. The thought was mine, the funds were worked out by the creativity of our clerk." I patted him on the back and walked away thinking I am beginning to understand what the General meant by, "What happens in Prison stays in Prison".

When I returned to my apartment there was a note on my door, that I had a package waiting for me at the Howard Post Office. I checked my pocket watch and I had about a half hour before the Post Office would close. It was a brisk walk, but I made it before closing time. It was a package from England. My parents must have shipped me a Christmas present. I arrived back at my apartment and began to open the box. A knock came at my door. I opened to discover Jim Anderson standing filling my doorway.

"Good afternoon Doctor. Sorry to disturb you. I just got off duty and I wanted to stop by, Georgiana and I would like to invite you to our home for Christmas. It would be nothing fancy. Just the children my wife and I. Nothing formal, Georgiana is making a ham with all the fixings. We understand if you already have plans." I thanked Jim and told him that I had no plans and would very much enjoy spending Christmas with his family. I told him that I was feeling a little down in the dumps, being away from family for the holidays, and spending Christmas with him and his family may be just what I needed.

"Dinner will be at 1:00pm, but feel free to come over and spend time with us and the children for some family time." I thanked him and shook hands, I was reminded of what a large man Jim is as my hand disappeared within his grip. You would never know that a short time ago he was lying on the ground with broken ribs.

Going back to my package I finished opening the box. Lying on top was a photograph of my mother and father dressed in their finest. They appeared much as I remember, a little older, but in good health. Neatly folded were a half dozen handkerchiefs that my mother had hand embroidered with my initials. Also there were two fine linen shirts with my initials embroidered on the right cuff, along with a half dozen pair of wool socks. In between the clothing was a small box. I opened it to find sweets, several pieces of English taffy, and dark chocolate. You cannot find sweets like these here, or I have not been able to find a shop that carried them. I thought I would bring a sample of them with me to the Andersons. They would enjoy a piece of England in their home, especially the children would enjoy stories of my homeland.

Christmas day arrived. I attended Christmas services at the Training School's Chapel. Reverend Nutting presided. A special treat was a concert by the boys' choir from the training school. The granite chapel with its dark wooden pews, brought me back to my childhood and the small church I would walk to with my mother and father, hand in hand, every Sunday morning. Those in attendance were a mix of male and female staff and the children who resided at the Training School. If I didn't know better, you would think that the gathering was made up of normal families in the neighborhood. Reverend Nutting made eye contact with me and he smiled a greeting to me. He is always pleased to see institutional staff in attendance at his services.

I arrived at the Andersons around 11:30am. The children were outside playing in the snow. I greeted them, and they ran to me greeting me with a hug, as if I were family. I must admit it brought a tear to my eye to be welcomed so warmly. I heard Jim call from the door way,

"Welcome Doctor. Now you children, don't be getting Doctor Jones all covered with snow." The children stepped back and I bent down and picked up a pile of snow and threw it at them. They squealed in delight and ran off into the yard. I joined Jim, brushing the snow from my top coat.

I could smell fresh baked goods as soon as I entered the home. My mind flashed back to my childhood home in England. "Welcome Doctor." I told Jim to call me Henry, and thanked him again for the invitation. "Join me in the parlor, Henry."

The parlor was larger than I thought it would be. In one corner there was a pine tree, decorated with mostly homemade decorations that appeared to have been made by the children. A garland made of popped corn and cranberries was strung from the branches. A fire burned in the fireplace across the room. The mantel was decorated with pine cones and candles. The room was comfortably furnished with sturdy oak furnishings similar to what furnished my apartment in the Resident Hall. Georgiana entered the room with a tray of Christmas cookies and a pot of tea. Both Jim and I stood to greet her.

She placed the tray down on the table in front of the couch. "I see you were able to rescue some cookies from the children," Jim told her. We laughed, and Georgiana welcomed me to their home. I told her that I hoped that I did not arrive too early. She assured me that I hadn't and we would be dinning around 1 o'clock. Georgiana excused herself and returned to the kitchen to finish the feast to come.

"So Jim, you are looking well. It appears that there are no lasting problems with your injuries?" He told me that he healed up fine except for a little stiffness in the cold. "That is to be expected with broken bones. They always come back to haunt you in bad weather." As we visited and shared small talk, the children came in from the cold. After removing their coats and boots they say cross legged in front of the fire place, warming themselves. "I have something for the children."

I went to my coat that was hanging on a hook in the front hall, and took a box from my front pocket. The children gathered around me as I sat back down on the couch. When I opened the box of sweets, their eyes grew wide with excitement. They looked at their father with questioning eyes. Jim told them that they could have some after dinner. Both of them drew deep breaths, smelling the sweet chocolates, and taffy from a faraway land.

We were summoned to the dining room by Georgiana. She had changed into a fresh holiday apron. I had never stopped to notice what a fine looking women she was. Her graying hair did not take away from her beauty and grace. She appeared small and petite, standing next to her large framed husband.

Jim was over six feet with wide shoulders and barrel chest. His upper arms stretched at the fabric of his shirt. A body that had known physical work all its life.

The table was long and was covered by a white tablecloth at each setting were matching plates and red napkins and what appeared to be silver knives forks and spoons. I complimented Georgiana on a fine table. Jim said, with a smile, that we don't get to see the good china and silver very often.

His wife, laughing told him, if she put it out every day he would break everything with his big mitts. Jim sat at the head of the table, His wife to his left. I was where she most likely sat at the other end of the table. The children took their places along the length of the table.

The vegetables and fresh warm rolls were already on the table. Georgiana went into the kitchen returning with the most beautiful large baked ham that I had ever seen. The meat was decorated with cherries and small crab apples. The platter had greens surrounding the ham, a large carving knife and fork rested the length of the platter.

Georgiana joined us at table and Jim asked that, as the guest of the family, if I would lead the family in giving thanks. I, along with the family all joined hands. "Blessed Lord, on this day of the celebration of the birth of your son Jesus, we give you thanks for all the blessings you have given myself and this family over the past year. We thank you for our health, especially for the recovery of your servant Jim; we thank you for a good harvest; and for the bounty spread out before us, of which we are about to partake. I thank you for this fine family who has welcomed me into their home, being far away from my family. Amen."

Following our fine dinner the family retired to the

parlor. Georgiana brought in a bowel of mulled cider. Jim added a little rum to the cups belonging to the adults. One of the children whispered something into the ear of their mother. She nodded her head and they ran to the table with the box that I had given them. Opening it they each selected a piece of the English candy. Jim and Georgiana shared a piece of taffy covered with dark chocolate. The commented that they had never had anything like it before. I smiled and told them that I had not been able to find any, even in the special candy shop in Providence.

I told the Andersons that I had a gift for them. I went to my coat again and this time returned with a package wrapped in green tissue paper, tied with red ribbon. I handed it to Georgiana, thanking her for all her efforts in making this Christmas very special to me. She carefully untied the ribbon and unfolded the paper. Inside she found my gift to the family. A first edition copy of Charles Dickens "A Christmas Carol" published in London in 1843, some fifty years ago. "I thought you and the children may enjoy the book. It is a story of its time in England, about conditions, the Cratchit Family the husband's Boss and visitations by several ghosts at Christmas. They said that they had heard of Dickens, but had not read any of his books, and thanked me. I found myself most comfortable with the Andersons. I was warm inside with the mulled cider and a touch of rum. A fine meal and being with family at this time of the year. Yes, family, because I now understand what the

Boss had meant when he told me that I was a part of the prison family. I had been welcomed to a new country by a tight knit group of people, who had accepted me. They viewed me as a member of their family and I saw them as my new family in America. The recent events I have experienced here in America and Rhode Island have been life changing. The people have become part of my new life and in essences my new family. And on this Christmas Day I thank my God for them and feel blessed.

WARDEN IN THE PRISON YARD

CHAPTER 9

DARK DAYS

Christmas was the high point of the year. The winter was especially cold and snowy. The gray stone walls and building of the Providence County Jail and the State Prison stood out against the white snow. When snow was falling the prison took on a ghostly appearance. Behind its walls the men wrapped themselves against the cold. Those with jobs within the prison looked forward to their work as a distraction to their living conditions. Others who were normally assigned to work in the fields of the prison farm or rented out to local farmers were confined to their cells except for meals and any odd jobs that the guards may find for them to do. Crews were sent to shovel snow other men were put on cleaning details to clean and disinfect the housing units, in attempts to control the spread of influenza among the prison population. The construction of the wooden barracks did help in reducing the overcrowded conditions. Also the fact that in the winter fewer crimes seemed to take place, except for the increase in commitments for public drunkenness. It appears to me, the local policemen take pity on the town drunkards in the winter, and by arresting them, secure for them food and shelter during the dead of winter.

I made it my habit to walk through each housing unit every other day to inspect for cleanliness and listen for signs of illness among the prisoners. Coughing and wheezing is an early indication that sickness maybe spreading within the population. I also check on the crews that are working on outdoor details. There is always a chance that in the cold and snow of frostbite setting into fingers and toes. Considering the winter we are having, those under my care are faring pretty well. Since early January we have had several days where temperatures fall below zero. No days have been above freezing. The old timers told me that normally there is a period of warmer weather in mid-January that they refer to as the January thaw. This year we have had no such luck.

I awoke on Monday January 29th not looking forward to my walk to the prison. Following my breakfast at the Staff Dinning Hall, I returned to my apartment to secure my medical bag before starting out to work. I was surprised by a knock at my door. I opened it to find the General, wrapped up in his heavy wool overcoat and high leather boots. "What a surprise, come in

Warden. What brings you out so early? Is everything alright? I asked. The Boss told me he was sorry to bother me so early, but Mary is not feeling well and he thought that she had a fever all night. He asked if I would stop and check on her before I went inside to work. "No trouble at all, Sir. I was not looking forward to the walk in this morning. Now I get to ride over with you, and check on how Mary is doing."

We descended the staircase to the front door. I could hear the wind howling and the snow was blowing across the road out of the north. The Warden's carriage was standing at the end of the walkway. Charlie must have removed the wheels and added the runners. The carriage was converted into a sleigh. We climb aboard, brushing snow from the leather seat, and headed to the main road leading to the prison. I normally would have walked across the railroad tracks as a short cut, waving as usual to the tower guards. But, the tracks had been plowed of snow and snow was piled about a meter, or three feet on both sides of the tracks blocking the sleigh's passage. We arrived at the warden's residence and the Boss pulled the sleigh up to the front door. His horse was breathing heavy and steam was rising from his old steed's back. The General called out to Charlie Brown, who was standing in the doorway of the carriage house, to come and tend to the horse. Charlie ran to us, and the Boss told him that he wouldn't be needing go anywhere for the rest of the day and he could put his horse up and clean off the carriage.

We entered the front door of the Warden's house, kicked the snow from our boots and hung our overcoats on the hooks in the hallway. "Mary!" the Boss called out for his wife. She called out to Nelson from the upstairs bedroom. "I have Doctor Jones with me. I asked him to make a visit to check on you before he went to his infirmary."

We climbed the staircase to the second floor. The Boss led the way to their bedroom. The door was closed and he knocked before opening it. Mary was seated on a chair, still in her nightdress wrapped with a blanked around her shoulders. I noticed her pale face and she was shivering slightly. I placed my medical bag on the small table by the bed, and felt her forehead. She was feverish. I took her pulse, it was strong and steady. A good sign. Opening my bag, I took out my stethoscope, putting the earpieces in my ears, I slid the other end between the buttons of Mary's nightdress to listen to her heart. She jumped as the end toughed her. I told her I was sorry, that I didn't think how cold it would be traveling outside all the way here. Her heart sounded strong, and I told her it sounded good. I listened to her back checking her lungs. There was a slight rattle indicating some congestion. I had her take several deep breaths, which caused her to start to cough. "Well Henry what do you think?" The Boss asked.

"Mary, your lungs seem to be congested and you have a fever. We don't want it developing into pneumonia. I will send over to the pharmacy for a jar of

Vicks Croup & Pneumonia Salve for you to put on your chest. It's a new product, breathing in the vapors and the warmth it gives to your chest will help your breathing. You should apply it twice a day, especially at bed time, it will help you sleep better through the night." I turned to the Warden.

"Nelson, I suspect you have a bottle of whiskey?" The Boss smiled, and said he was sure he had an old bottle somewhere around. "Well, I want you to make up a nice hot toddy. My old college professor gave me a recipe that he said was the only good thing to come out of Ireland in a hundred years." I wrote down the mixture for him. Everything you need, except the whiskey the kitchen will have, I will have the Chief Steward send what you need out. Serve it warm, it has onions for vitamin C, for health. I would prefer lemon but this time of the year they are hard to come by. Honey to soothe, the whiskey is to numb. She should drink it before bed for the next two nights. Oh Nelson, I'm sure if you join her in a cup, it won't hurt you." Mary laughed a little causing her to cough. "I will stop back at the end of the day to check on you. I want you to stay in bed. Don't worry about the Boss he, can fend for himself for a few days, right General?" The Boss shook my hand and thanked me for coming. He assured me that he would make sure she stayed in bed and rested.

I told the Warden that I would let myself out, and proceeded into the prison. Frank and Ed were in the hallway outside their offices. I stopped to greet them.

The Deputy looked at his watch and noted that I was running a little late today. I told him that I had to make a visit to the Warden's Residence, but never mentioned that Mary was not feeling well. I headed out the heavy steel door into the prison yard and headed to the Infirmary. Snow was swirling around at my feet as I walked past the wooden barracks and on to the white stucco building. I banged on the door and the officer opened it allowing me in. "Sure is cold out there this morning Doc." The Guard pulled his pocket watch out. "Running a little late today. Must have been a cold walk in today." I gave no explanation for being late, nor did I mention that I road in with the Warden.

Jails and Prisons both run on a time schedule. Everything has it time and place. I never gave it much thought, until it was noted twice that I was later than my usual time. "I have the men for the medication line all ready for you. Let me know when you are ready to start and I will send them in to see you." The prisoners in the ward have already eaten. They all seem in good shape to me, so take your time, Doc." I thanked him and saw to the prisoners there for sick call.

The day passed uneventfully. I left the infirmary and decided to work my way through the barracks and cell houses to assess the conditions. Again all seemed in order. Oscar Kemp, one of the cell block officer called me over to his desk. "Doctor, can you do me a favor? My daughter has been suffering from a heavy cough for two days now and it seems to be keeping her up all night. Would you have a chance to take a look at her?" I asked if she seemed to be running a fever. "No, my wife has been watching for that." I can see her late this afternoon. If you or your wife can bring her by the Residence Hall around six o'clock, I will check her over, I told him. I gave him some comfort, and told him that I thought that she was going to be fine, seeing that there was no fever. "Thanks Doctor, I will bring her by. You're a fine man. What will the visit be? I will want to pay you for your time." I assured him there would be no charge. We shook hands and I continued on my rounds. Everything seemed to be in good order. A mild smell of disinfectant was evident as I walked through the units.

After checking out with Deputy Slocum, I went to the Boss's house to check on Mary. The Warden was just leaving his upstairs office and we walked together to the house. "I checked on my wife around 12:30, she seemed to be resting comfortably." I told him I was glad to hear that. "The Vicks stuff seemed to help her breath better." I said that I have been impressed with the product for a while and have prescribed it on a number of occasions. Many times I have ordered it for children even babies. We entered the house and hung our coats up, then climbed the stairs to the bedroom.

We entered, Mary smiled when she saw her husband and me. "How is my patient doing?" I asked. She shook her head and said softly that she was not doing too well. I set my bag down and took out my stethoscope, placing the ear pieces in my ears I took the other end between my hands and blew on it to warm it. Mary smiled, and I gave her a wink of the eye, and smiled. I listened to her heart and lungs, then checked for fever. Her heart sounded strong but the lungs seemed to be more congested. She was feverish, and her skin was clammy and damp with sweat.

"How has the coughing been?" Both her and her husband said it seemed better. I told them to continue with the Vicks and the hot toddy at bed time. "We need to bring your fever down. Warden, after I leave if you could bathe Mary in cool water. That should help with the fever and will make her feel better cooling the skin." I told them that I would stop in again early in the morning. "If anything should happen during the night, don't hesitate to send for me and I will come right away." I said goodbye, and the Boss walked me out of the room, and down the stairs. He asked me if she was going to be alright. "I am concerned. I am worried about her lungs and pneumonia setting in. She has a good strong heart and that is always a good sign. If we can't clear the lungs we may have to bring her into the hospital for oxygen treatment. We will have a better idea in the morning. Let us wait and see what the morning brings." The Boss thanked me and I headed back to my apartment.

On the way home I stopped at the dining hall for dinner. I had a bowl of beef stew and some cornbread. It really hit the spot on a cold evening. When I arrived at the Resident Hall, I found Doctor Bill McCaw seated in the parlor with drink in hand. I joined him, "What a surprise. You are usually on your way back to Providence by now." He asked if I wanted a drink. "Yes that would be nice on a cold evening." I sat with him and he told me, that the General had sent word to him that Mary was not feeling well. "Yes she is very congested and feverish. Her heart seems strong, but I am concerned about pneumonia. This year's influenza that is going around can be a bitch."

Bill sat thoughtfully, and then asked if there was anything he could do to help. I knew that the Boss had asked him for advice. "Bill, don't feel like you are interfering with my patient and I. I am the new Doctor. You have been the only Doctor for the prison for many years. The General has a great deal of trust and confidence in you, and after all we are talking about the Boss's wife." I took a sip of my drink. "Tomorrow, if there is no improvement, I was going to have Mary admitted to the hospital for oxygen treatment. If you are agreeable I would like to suggest to the General that we have her admitted to Rhode Island Hospital in Providence. You have privileges there, and I think she would be better off there than at the hospital here at the Institutions. Also being the Warden's wife, everyone here will know all their business. Things would be a lot more private for them at the city hospital. I will recommend to the General that you be brought in on her case, and we will consult on any treatment." Bill nodded his head, as we touched glasses, to seal the agreement. "There is no reason for the General or Mary to know that we talked this evening. Let it be my suggestion to call you in. I don't want the General to feel embarrassed that he talked to you about Mary's illness behind my back. I understand you have many years more experience in medicine than I, and a special relationship over the years with him and Mary." We shook hands, just as the Kemp family entered the residence. "I have a patient to see, Bill. I will get back to you tomorrow on Mary's condition." He said see you later, go take care of your patient Doctor.

I greeted the Kemp family. "Mr. and Mrs. Kemp, nice to see you. And who is this young lady?" Oscar told me that his daughter's name was Ida. Well, Ida I am Doctor Jones and your father and I work together. He told me that you were not feeling well. How about you and your mother and father come up stairs and I can see if I can help you feel better." We climbed the staircase and walked to my room. We entered, "Ida have a seat here by the window, near the lamp." I opened my bag and took out the tools I thought I would use and put them on the small table that the lamp was on. Ida looked the items over nervously. "Now Dad have a seat on the couch and Mommy come over here with us. I picked up the stethoscope and showed it to Ida. This is to listen to your heart and lungs. I put the ear pieces into her ears and let her listen to her mother's heart beating. She smiled and told her mother what she heard. "Now I need to hear your heart. Now turn around so I can listen to your back. That's it, now take a deep breath, good, again, good. Now I need to look into your ears." I tilted her head from side to side allowing the light to shine into the ear canals. "Good, I was told that you have a sore throat. Is that right?" She nodded and coughed a yes in response. "Well, let me take a look." I picked up a wooden tongue depressor, and showed it to her. "This is to keep your tongue out of the way so I can see down your throat." I took from my bag a small bottle containing honey. This was a trick my Doctor used on me when I was small. I put a few drops of honey on both sides of the tongue depressor. "Now open wide and say ahrr." Holding her tongue down, I looked into her throat. "That's good, alright now." I gave her the tongue depressor and she licked the honey off the stick. I told Ida's mother that it just appeared irritated from all the coughing she has been experiencing. There did not appear to be any infection. "I think just resting the throat and coating it to protect the surface will take care of it." I opened the draw of my desk and took out three pieces of orange hard candy. "I think I have just the right medicine for you, Ida." I handed the girl the candy. "Now I want you to have one of these today after dinner. Don't chew it just suck on it until it is gone. The other two, take one after your lunch and one after dinner tomorrow the same way. That should take care of you sore throat." She took the candy and looked up at her mother. Her mother just nodded to her and told her to thank the Doctor, which she did. "Now mommy, I want you to give Ida a teaspoon of honey at bed time tonight. Also some warm tea and honey with breakfast in the morning. She should be fine. If she isn't better in a couple of days, bring her back to me. But, she should be fine." The whole family thanked me as they left my apartment. I told Oscar that I would see him at work in the morning and see how she is doing.

In the morning after some breakfast at the Dining Hall, I headed down the hill and across the tracks to the prison. The weather had improved, the sun was shining, bright blue sky and little or no wind to speak of. It had warmed up a bit and the walk in was brisk but not unpleasant. I waived my usual wave to the tower guards as I passed and went directly to the Warden's Residence. I knocked at the front door. The door opened. The Boss was standing there in his shirtsleeves, and asked me in. "How did the night go, General?" He told me it was a long night for the both of them. He had done as instructed trying to cool her off and applied the Vicks as I told him. "Nelson, can we have a talk before I go check on Mary?" He led me into the kitchen and took a seat at the table. I joined him. General, I have to tell you that I am worried about Mary and her lack of improvement. I have given it a lot of thought overnight, and I decided that if I found no improvement this morning, I was going to ask for your permission to call in Doctor McCaw to consult on Mary's condition.

He has a great deal more experience than I, and also has admitting privileges at Rhode Island Hospital in the city. If we have to admit her, I feel that she would be better off there, rather than here at the institutions." The Boss looked into my eyes for a few seconds. I noticed his eyes water up a little as he stood up, looking away. He said that whatever I recommended him to do he would do. "Good, good, even if we don't need to admit Mary into the hospital, with you and Mary's permission I would like to call Doctor McCaw for his opinion." Whatever you think is best, Henry he said. "Let us go see Mary and how she is doing."

The General gave a knock on the door and we entered the bedroom. "Well, how is my favorite patient doing this morning?" She shook her head, and said not well, not well at all. "Let me get a look at you. General could you open the drapes and let the sun in. It is a beautiful morning outside today." The room lit up with sunlight as the drapes were pull open. She sat up a little in the bed she knew the routine and wanted to make my examination easier for me. I listened to her heart and lungs, her body was still feverish and she had developed a raspy cough. "Well, Mrs. Viall, we need to discuss our next move." She looked up at her husband. "I think I need a little help with your condition. I would like, your permission, to consult with our old friend Doctor McCaw. He has many more years of experience than I, and I value his opinion. If you and the General agree, I will contact him this morning and have him stop over to have a look at you." Again she looked to her husband. They nodded to each other, and Mary told me that if I thought it best, I could call in Doctor Bill to check on her. "Very good, then I will get a hold of him. He should have already arrived on the morning train, and have him stop by." I shook hands with the Boss and gave Mary a hug. The Warden escorted me to the door. He told me how worried he was about her and didn't know what he would ever do without her. "Let us not be thinking the worse, she is a strong woman and has a lot of fight in her. She has to, to take care of you." The General laughed and patted me on the back as I was leaving. "Can I send Charlie Brown up to the hospital with a note to Doctor McCaw?" The warden told me to let Ed now that I was sending him, so no one thinks he ran away. I told the Deputy and gave Charlie the note to Bill and sent him on his way.

Latter in the day, one of the guards came into the infirmary and told me that the Warden had request that I report to his house. It was about 2:45 in the afternoon. I told the officer in the infirmary that I may not be back today, and left for the Warden's Residence. I arrived and knocked. I was not surprised to see Doctor McCaw when I entered. "Bill, thank you for coming so quickly." He told me that he had been here for a while and had already examined Mary. "What do you think?" He told me that she is a very sick woman and that I have done everything that he or I can do for her at her home. He said that in his opinion she needed to be hospitalized. "That is my recommendation also. Have you told her?" Bill indicated that he had only told the Warden what he recommended. And, being my patient it was up to me to make the decision and to inform her of it. "Gee thanks." Bill smiled. "Alright let us go and give her the news." The Warden told us that she won't be happy to leave the house, but she knows that she is very sick and that a hospital is where she needs to be. The three of us entered the bedroom.

Mary looked at the three of us and knew that a decision had been made to send her to the hospital. "Well, gentlemen, when do I need to go to the hospital?" We all looked at each other. "Doctors, Nelson knows I am not a stupid woman. I know what needs to be done and that you all are acting in my best interest. So when and where will I be going? The General laughed out loud and gave Mary a hug. I told her that I thought that going into the city to Rhode Island Hospital would be the best place. And that Doctor McCaw would oversee her care there because his home and office is in Providence close by. Also, for the hospital records, Doctor McCaw will be her primary Physician. "Good, I didn't think I wanted to be at the hospital here at the institutions. Too many wagging tongues knowing our business." We all laughed, even Mary causing her to go into a coughing fit.

It was Tuesday February 2th 1894 when we transported Mary to Rhode Island Hospital. The day was sunny and warmer than normal. The Warden and Bill

McCaw accompanied her on the trip by carriage from Cranston to Providence. I patted her hand as they were ready to leave and told her not to give the nurses a bad time. She smiled and nodded in agreement. Little did any of us know that she would never again set foot in the Warden's Residence.

As feared, pneumonia had set into her lungs. Even with oxygen treatment she had great difficulty breathing. Bill updated me every morning on her condition. The Warden spent most of his time at the hospital by her side. Deputy Slocum took care of business at the prison. I visited Mary every other day, reading her medical charts and talking to Bill and her nurses. By Sunday the seventh she had lapsed into a comma. Prayers were offered by Reverend Nutting in the prison chapel.

On Monday morning as I was about to head out to the prison, there was a knock on my apartment door. I opened to see Bill McCaw. I knew what he was about to tell me. He came into the room and told me that "your patient Mary W. Viall had quietly passed away at 3:08 this morning." I asked if the Boss had been told yet. "He was there with her all night. I sent for him around 11:00pm last night. It didn't look good and I thought that he would want to be with her." I thanked him for all that he had done.

"Henry, this is going to be very hard on the General. As tough as you think he is, she was his life. He is not going to handle this well. She is all he had outside of being Warden. They had lost all their children at a very young age. He is now left alone to deal with his demons, and I am afraid for him. Keep a close eye on him, and spend time talking with him as a friend, more than his physician.

There was black bunting over the doorway to the Warden's Residence. The wake and funeral was private. Reverend Nutting presided over the service. There were several members of Mary's family from Connecticut there, along with myself, Bill McCaw and the inner circle of prison staff. Mary was buried in the family plot at the Lakeside – Carpenter Cemetery in East Providence. The Monument read, "Mary W. Viall, Died February 8, 1894, Age 64 Years".

On Monday morning, following the funeral I stopped at the Warden's house to see how the General was doing. I knocked at the door several times. There was no answer. I was worried at first, but just assumed that the Boss had gone into the prison earlier than usual. I stopped at Frank's office to inquire how the Boss was doing. "The Warden was in early this morning and addressed the staff at roll call." He then met with me and Ed. He asked us to tell you, when you arrived, that he would be taking some time off. The Deputy will be in command until he returns." I asked him, when the General planned to return? "He didn't say. We didn't think it was wise to ask. If he wanted us to know he would have told us. He did ask that you inform Dr. Keene and the Chairman of the Board that he was taking some time away to grieve the loss of his wife, and he would stay in contact with Deputy Slocum." In the back of my mind, I was worried about him. The General is a strong man but this is a traumatic event for him especially at his age. "So Doctor, you will take care of notifying the people on the hill?" I told Frank that I would see Doctor Keene this afternoon, and he will take care of the notification to the Board. As I was leaving Frank's office I ran into the Deputy, and asked him how the Boss looked this morning. Ed said he looked fine as always, seemed steady as a rock and in control. I asked if he expected anything less. He smiled and told me that he has seen him in the middle of the yard with rioting prisoners as calm as if he were standing at a church service. We both shook our heads smiling.

The week passed as usual. Come Friday, again I was getting concerned not having any word on the Boss or when he may return. Late Friday evening I was relaxing in my apartment when a knock at my door startled me. I opened to find Ed Slocum standing there. "Ed what a surprise. What can I do for you?" He asked if he could come in that there is a problem with the General. "Oh my God! Is he alright?" Ed told me, yes and no. "What is going on?" The Chief of Police in Providence got a hold of me, he said. "Come on man, come on, what happened?"

Ed went on to tell me that, the General was drunk and causing some problems at the GAR Lodge he belongs. He has been living in a spare room at the Lodge since Monday. The Post Commander is a friend of the Chiefs and he asked for help with the boss trying to keep things quiet and get help controlling him. Ed went on, it appears things were going along alright until the General started shooting the lights out in the room because he could walk to turn them off. "Where is he now?" The Deputy said that he called his nephew Frank and they went to the Lodge and picked him up. The Police Chief was a big help and would keep a lid on what happened. We brought him back to the prison and put him to bed. He told me that Frank was with him now. "Ed, let me get some things together and I will go with you and check him over." The Deputy thanked me and we set out to the prison.

We arrived at the Warden's house and went inside. Frank was sitting in the parlor. "Hello Frank, where is he?" He said that he was upstairs in bed and was sleeping it off. He thanked me for coming. I told them. "We are going to need to watch him for a while. This loss is going to be very hard on him. We don't want him doing something stupid and ruining his reputation, or, God forbid, taking his own life." Frank spoke up and said, you don't think he would do something like that do you Doc? "You know him better than me, Frank, but with alcohol and being depressed, people can do things totally out of their normal character." We went upstairs to check on him. He seemed to be sleeping quietly. The room smelled of whiskey and body odor. He had several day old beard and his hair was matted to his head. If we didn't know it was him, we would have had difficulty recognizing him.

"What do you think Henry?" Ed asked. "Do you think we should just leave and let him sleep it off?" I told them that in my opinion he should not be left alone until he regains control of himself. "Do you think I should have an officer assigned to the house?" I told the Deputy that I didn't think that that was a good idea, the General would never want his business the talk of the prison. "Doc, I hate to ask, but could you stay here with him for a while? Just to watch over his medical condition of course." I told Ed and Frank that I thought that that would be a good idea, and even the General could be convinced it is for the best. "Good, then it is done, Frank and I will head home and you will stay and watch over him. If you need anything just let me know in the morning. We will all get him through this. We will keep tonight to ourselves, and as the Boss always says, "What happens in prison stays in prison."

I set myself up in a small guest room down the hallway from the Warden's room. In the morning I heard him get out of bed and enter the hall outside his room. I didn't want to startle him so I quietly called to him from inside the room. "Who is it? Who is here?" I told him it's Henry, Henry Jones. He opened the door to the guest room. "Doctor, what are you doing here?" I told him that, I needed a place to stay for the night and didn't think he would mind if I stayed with him.

He looked at me questioning what he had just heard. Then as it sunk into his cloudy alcohol dazed mind what I had said, he broke out into a big belly laugh. And grabbed his head. "Oh God Henry, don't make me laugh my head hurts." I suggested to the Boss that he get cleaned up and I would put the coffee pot on, and meet him in the kitchen. He agreed and I went down to the Kitchen. I looked out the window and saw Chief Steward Towne walking to the prison entrance. It had to be around 5:15am. I called to him through the back kitchen door, and asked that he send some breakfast out for the Warden and me. He asked everything was alright. I assured him we were fine. He didn't pursue the matter further.

I went through the kitchen cupboard and found the can of tea that Mary had, and put the pot on next to the Boss's coffee pot. In about a half hour the General came into the kitchen, commenting on how good the coffee smelled. "You smell better also." He smiled sheepishly. "How are you feeling Warden?" He commented that he was a little better now that he is cleaned up.

"General we have to talk." He asked that I fill him in on what happened and why I was here at his house. "Do you remember anything from last night?" He shook his head and said that the last he knew it was Wednesday and he was staying at the lodge. "Let me bring you up to date." I told him. "Today is Saturday. Last night Ed and Frank brought you home from the Lodge out cold drunk. The Chief of Police contacted

Ed to come and get you that you had caused a problem at the Lodge and the Post Commander was concerned for you." What did I do? "You shot out the lights in the room you were staying in."

Oh no, he said as he shook his head. I'm in a world of shit now he exclaimed.

"No, it was taken care of. Ed spoke to the Commander and the Police Chief. Everything is alright as if nothing happened. Ed reminded the Commander that the Post was named after his father and your heroic commander, and how would it look that a past Commander of the GAR was arrested." Shaking his head the Warden said he would go and apologize to the Chief and Commander in person. "They were worried when they got you home and came for me to make sure you were going to be alright. That is about it and here we are now having breakfast together." He thanked me, just as a kitchen inmate arrived with some corn muffins and preserves. We thanked him and sent him back to the kitchen.

"Warden it is my recommendation, as your Doctor, and I hope friend, that I remain here with you for a while. It would be good for me also. It is a cold walk to the prison every day. What do you think?" The General walked around the table and poured another cup of coffee. He sat down and asked if he had a choice. "Of course you have a choice, you're the Boss. This is your house and I work for you, Sir." He thought for a few minutes and said that a smart man should always follow recommendations of those people who watches out for your best interest. "I guess that we are going to be roommates for a little while then Warden."

Call me Nelson while we are here alone, alright Henry? He said. After our breakfast I went inside to the Infirmary. As I passed Frank Viall's office he asked if everything was alright. I just nodded and continued on my way.

I went out to the Warden's house at lunch time just to see how the Boss was doing. He was seated in the parlor with a drink in his hand. He was still sober and drinking from a glass. I took that as an improvement. "How you doing, Nelson? A little of the dog that bit you?" He smiled and said that he was wondering what he was going to say to the GAR Post Commander, after making such a fool of himself. "Look, Nelson, those gentlemen have all known you for many years. And after what you have been through for the past couple of weeks, your drunken escapade will be excused." He told me that he was going to go to the lodge this afternoon and square things up with them, and try to see the Police Chief while he is in the city.

"How are things inside? I need to thank Frank and Ed for their help last night." I told him that all is well and I never heard a peep of a rumor of what had happened. "Frank and Ed are good men. They will keep everything to themselves." Did you get any questions about you staying here come up?" I told him that I brought it up before anyone asked. "What did you tell them?" I told everyone what a great guy you are to allow me to stay with you so I didn't have to walk into the prison in the dark, snow and cold every morning. "And they believed that I was that kind? Doctor, be careful you will be ruining my reputation." We laughed.

"I have to be getting back to my patients. If you do decide to go to the city. You should make this your last drink for the afternoon. We don't want them getting the wrong idea." The Boss told me that this was it for the day, and he would be dressing up to make his apologies. We shook hands and I headed back to the Infirmary for my afternoon medical line.

By Monday February 19th I was getting very worried about the Boss. Most nights he would pass out and fall asleep in the parlor chair. I awoke that morning and quietly passed the General's bedroom door. I didn't want to wake him. I quietly went down the stairs and headed to the kitchen. From the hallway I could see the General sitting at the kitchen table with his back towards me. I was surprised he was up so early. I quietly walked down the hall to the door way.

That is when I noticed that in front of him on the table was left to right, his Warden's Badge, a bottle of whiskey and his pistol by his right hand. I dared not to startle him. He may turn and I could die where I stood. I quietly watched from behind. He sat quietly just staring off into nothing ness. As I watched he slowly stood up and put his badge into his left pocket, put the pistol into his right pocket and picked up the bottle and walked to the sink. He proceeded to pour the remainder down the drain. He turned and saw me standing in the door way. "Good morning Henry. How are you this morning?" I replied, that I was fine, and how are you doing? He told me. "I am much better this morning. It is time to get back to work." We sat together over breakfast silent for a few minutes.

Doctor, thank you for all your help and support over the past couple of weeks. Loosing Mary has been very difficult for me. I didn't think I could live without her or if I wanted to. But it's time to saddle up and get back to work, so to speak. I will be riding the wall this morning, then heading to my office. When you go in please ask the Deputy to meet me in my office in an hour."

And Henry, tell Frank to put the word out that I will be needing a house keeper, unless you want to change jobs, Doctor?" I laughed and shook my head. "Good, good, you are a much better Doctor and friend than you would be a house keeper. Once I employ someone, Henry you can move back to your apartment. I need to get accustomed to living alone. But, thank you for staying with me through this." I went to work and followed the Boss's orders and told Ed and Frank what he had said, with a big smile on my face and a much liter heart. What I had observed in the kitchen that morning I never spoke of it to anyone, not even the Warden. What happens in prison stays in prison.

CHAPTER 10
Change comes slowly

The General has hired a housekeeper to keep the home fires burning. I should say that he has hired several housekeepers. Most only remained a few weeks or even days. His new housekeeper, Maureen is the widow of a prison officer Richard Flynn, who had passed away. She has two small children and was having some trouble making ends meet. Frank Viall had recommended her to the Boss. I met her the other morning when I stopped in the General's office to discuss eliminating the use of straightjackets as a part of discipline for unruly prisoners. The practice is causing some to have permanent injuries. Also placing a prisoner on a diet of bread and water should be discontinued.

I don't think I will ever get use to going to the Warden's office. The large oak door has you intimidated before you even knock for entrance. I feel like a boy going to the headmaster's office when I was in primary school in England. I knocked and the door opened immediately startling me. It was the new housekeeper. She happened to be bringing the Boss another pot of coffee. "Come in Doctor, I'd like you to meet my new housekeeper Maureen Flynn. Maureen this is our Doctor, Henry Jones." I reached out for her hand and she gave a small curtsy.

"How nice to meet you, Doctor. I was just bring the Warden a pot of coffee. Would you like a cup?" The Boss told Maureen that I was an Englishman and may prefer some tea. Maureen told me that, "I came from County Kildare, Ireland, when I was just a girl, and married my late husband, Richard. The Lord took him last year. It's just me and my two children now." I noticed her eyes tearing up as she turned away from me. "I will bring you your tea, Doctor Jones." Just a cup would be fine, I told her that I would share the pot of coffee with the General. The Boss laughed.

"You may want the tea, Doctor. I take my coffee as black and as strong as my heart."

Maureen responded saying that, "'Tis true, Doctor, I don't know how he can drink it. I don't think he is a black'arted man, my Richard always spoke well of the Warden, and he has been nothing but a gentleman to me the last few days. I will bring you your tea." She again curtsied and left the office closing the door.

"Well Doctor what brings you here so early?" I told the Warden that I wanted to speak to him about the practice of using a straightjacket for long periods of time, on unruly prisoners, also placing them on just bread and water rations while in the "Black Cells". "Doctor, you know that this is a prison and we houses many violent and dangerous men. We do have to maintain order. There has to be consequences for violating the prison rules. There has to be a deterrent to bad behavior. This is not a boarding school or a hospital. Even the asylum makes use of the straightjacket on some of its patients."

"I understand that the Asylum still uses it. But only for a short period of time to prevent the patient from injuring themselves. It is not used as punishment. I have seen several cases, in my short time here, where the prisoner has taken over a week, or in some cases a month to recover from long periods of confinement in one of them. One inmate I saw last week will be permanently disabled from the thirty days he spent in the jacket. It caused traumatic neuritis of the shoulders which, because of its excruciating pain, and brought them to the sick line for months."

A knock came at the office door. I opened it to find Maureen with a tray with a tea pot and cup. I was so intent on making my case with the Boss, I had forgotten that she was bringing tea. "Thank you Maureen." I took the tray from her and thanked her as she closed the door behind herself. I placed the tray on a table and poured myself a cup. The Warden and I both took a sip of our drinks.

He was looking me straight in the eyes as he drank his coffee. It was as if he was reading my mind searching for some ulterior motive for my concern. I dared not to look away. As it would signal that I was intimidated by his look.

"Well, Doctor, I will take your concerns under advisement and will get back to you on this matter. The injuries you described does affect the prisoners ability to engage in productive work, and its rehabilitative results. What else seems is on your mind? You had mentioned there were a couple of things you wanted to talk to me about?"

"The practice of putting a prisoner on bread and water as their only form of subsistence while in segregation cells. As the prison physician, It is hard for me to accept the idea of any prisoner being reformed by starvation, or depriving the body of those necessary, chemically vital food constituents which formed and made the body. The health of the prisoners must be maintained, for the environment and their psychology. The practice tends to lower normal resistance and render them prey to diseases such as tuberculosis." The Boss stood up and walked to the window. He looked out across a freshly plowed field in the early May morning. It seemed like several minutes before he turned towards me, taking another sip of his coffee.

"Is there anything else our Doctor has on his mind?" I did but this wasn't the time to bring additional changes up. I was once told you don't eat an elephant all at once. You need to take one bite at a time. I told the Boss that that was what I wanted to talk about today. "I will think about your concerns and make a decision over the next week or so. I will get back to you on our discussion. In the mean time I hope that our meeting will remain between us. It would be a mistake if the prisoners or staff hear of your concerns.

Back in '80 I abolished the use of corporal punishment here. I received a great deal of pushback from other State Wardens and the Adjutant of the State Militia. It was a big change in what was considered necessary to maintaining discipline in the military and a prison. I myself resorted to the lash with my colored troops in Mississippi that mutinied. They could have been shot for their actions." I told the Boss that I understood and look forward to his decision.

I put my cup down on the tray. "Warden, Thank you for giving me the opportunity to meet with you on these matters. I understand that change does not come easy within a prison, and I appreciate your consideration." As I closed the office door and started down the stairs, I was hopeful for a positive decision. I had tried to point out to the Boss the advantages to the prison operation and most of all production improvements from prisoner labor.

During the Warden's tour of the prison, I noticed that he was spending more time than usual talking to the prisoners even those being segregated for rule infractions. As I remember, about ten days or so following our talk the Boss called a meeting of the command staff. I was included in the meeting. My attendance became common place over the years. The Deputy and each of the shift commanders along with the Chief Steward were present. Frank Viall and the Reverend Nutting were also invited. The presents of the Chaplin was a surprise to everyone.

When the General entered everyone became quiet and the custody staff came to attention. "Gentlemen, please be seated. Thank you all for coming. I wanted to call you all together to make a few announcements regarding some operational changes I have decided to make." The Boss took his seat and took several papers from his desk drawer. "First of all, I have been given some good news by our Chief Clerk. We have entered into two new contracts with private companies. One is a garment company that has purchased shirts made by our prisoners. This company has been impressed with the quality of the work and had doubled its order this year. The other is a new company selling shoes and other leather goods.

In light of these new contracts we need to increase our production. You are all aware that the profits from inmate labor goes a long way in offsetting our operational cost. We are close to completely covering our operational cost through prison industries." He paused and looked around the room. "As you may have noticed I have been a lot more visible lately and have been talking to our industrial staff, prison officers and prisoners.

And I will be announcing several changes that I believe will increase productivity and man power.

I called you together to give you advanced notice of the changes: 1. the policy of prisoners being restrained in straightjackets as punishment will be amended. The items will only be used to control violent aggressive prisoners until such time they have calmed themselves. There use will be limited to 24 hours. The prison physician will examine the prisoner within 24 hours of application and his approval is necessary to continue its use. I have noticed that the practice we have been using of long term use has been causing the prisoner to be unable to work for a long period of time following the removal. 2. I will be changing the practice of placing prisoners on rations of bread and water while being held in solitary confinement will be discontinued. The prisoners will be put on reduced rations, of two meals a day without a desert course. Should the prisoner throw or destroy their rations, they will be placed on bread and water for 48 hours or until they comply with the reduced meals. Both of these changes will go into effect next Monday morning. Effective the first of next month I have received approval from the Board to pay inmates a small incentive pay based upon production. This should encourage the prisoners to increase production, which will offset the cost of being paid. Our Chief Clerk will monitor our production and production costs for ninety days and prepare a report for me to present to the Board on the effectiveness of the incentive pay. Are there any questions?"

Everyone looked at one another. The Deputy raised his hand. He stood and informed the Warden, "These changes will not sit well with some of the staff. They will feel that their authority is being reduced and the changes are coddling the prisoners."

I couldn't help but think to myself, the General is a genius of a tactician. I now understand his tenure of thirty years as Warden. With the Board of Charity and Corrections and the State Legislature, his manner, his fearlessness, his War record, and his common sense was the key to their unlocking the doors for whatever appropriations he needed. Being careful and frugal by nature, he kept the prison as nearly self-supporting as possible. His methods of good order and discipline, his modes of farming were held up as a model to the other superintendents adjoining him. The resulting jealously and strife were prominent. With his beliefs on strict standing on property rights, took the place of useful and neighborly coordination with the other superintendents.

On one side was a group of institutions, with strict discipline as a reformatory method. On the other side, the mental and physical divisions were greatly interested in neither reform nor discipline. Their interests were focused on physical well-being of their charges. They found their methods subject to the scrutiny and criticism of the Board favorable to the State Prison. The Warden's productive management was constantly held before them as an example of good institutional management.

At time, under the guise of occupational therapy, the prison labor, turned a substantial profit in such occupations as shirt making. Ventures such as this impressed and gave political cover to elected officials for approving costs of modern improvements at the prison. I had experienced a number of inmate suicides that I suspected was brought about by the stress. Too much stress may have been put on the prisoner in order to make him a more productive worker in the shirt shop. I had brought this to the Boss's attention following the suicide. The new policy of payment to the prisoners for extra work the prisoner would feel less of a slave and have him make a high mark in production. The end result the General maintains his reputation with the Board and the Legislature as a tough, law and order prison administrator while bringing much needed improvements to the prison.

"Ed, that's why I have brought you all together. I am counting on you all to support the changes I am making. The changes being made does not reduce the guard's authority. Their authority is given them by me. I share my authority with them. I'm the Warden and I'm the Boss. The increase in production I hope to attain will also help me to fund pay increases for the staff. Let that sink into their thick heads." There were some laughs around the room.

"This is the time of year we need every prisoner

working. The farm is ready for planting, the grounds need work and our industries are in full operation. I want to get the runners out working also as field hands. They will remain in red suits to identify them as escape risk. They should also understand, that should they again attempt escape, the guards are authorized to shoot them."

That brought to mind that on one occasion the Warden going into the prison yard alone, he noticed a prisoner scaling the wall. He allowed the prisoner to climb to the top. He fired, knocking the cement and stones into the prisoner's face. He fell like a log on the ground. Walking over to the prisoner he asked, while pointing his smoking revolver at him, "What are you trying to do Charlie?" The Boss brought him to me in the infirmary to tend to his injuries and then a segregation cell.

Without any further comments, the Warden ended the meeting. Several of those present gathered into small groups talking. I went to the Boss and thanked him for his decision. He smiled. He said, "Sometimes change can be good for everyone."

For the rest of the week the prison was abuzz with talk about the changes. Most of the staff were supportive of the changes. Those that did not, changed their minds after a talk with Deputy Slocum. One hard liner resigned from the prison. The inmates that I saw in the medical line asked me how the Warden came up with the changes. I gave them the party line. "This is about dollars and cents, the Warden expects you to do all you can to increase production. It's good for you and it's good for the prison and good for the staff. His decision can make things better for everyone." I added that even I benefit with fewer prisoners at sick call, and they would laugh.

On one occasion I was asked to give a lecture at Brown University about prison reform and society. The class had students of sociology, psychology and penology. The lecture hall was full. My lecture lasted an hour. A number of students remained following my talk to ask questions about how is was to work behind the prison wall with dangerous criminals all around. One of the students told me that he was studying penology and was wondering if it was possible to work in the prison over the summer and during breaks in classes. I told him that the Warden is always looking for good men to staff the prison. Especially at this time of the year it would be a good time to apply. I told him to go to the prison and fill out an application. He asked me if he could mention my name as the person who informed him of the job possibility. I told him I was fine about that, but not knowing him, I could not formally recommend him for a position. He did apply and after an interview with the Warden he was hired on the first of June, to work until after the harvest, the end of September.

One day this student was assigned to tower duty on the west wall. It was a warm September afternoon, when sleep over-powering him after his noon meal. Suddenly he was brought awake by revolver shots and bullets crashing through the window of the tower house, barely missing his head. Rushing out on the wall, rifle in hand he found the Warden sitting in his covered-top buggy just alongside the wall, with a smoking pistol in his hand. The Boss asked the guard if he had been sleeping, and warned him to get to bed earlier and he wouldn't be so drowsy. Not a word was said about discharging him nor did the Warden discharge him for being asleep on duty. It was the student who told me what had happened and he promised to never fall asleep on the job again, and hoped that I didn't get in trouble for his actions, as he had mentioned my name when he applied. I informed him I hadn't heard anything about it and didn't expect to, The Boss took care of it, so there is no need for anyone else to be involved. Although he did hear from Frank Viall the Chief Clerk that the cost of repairing the window that he had accidently broke in the tower was deducted from his pay that month.

The fall and winter passed without any major problems. That winter was fairly mild. We did have snow, but mostly it was just an annoyance. Two or three inches at a time, a couple of times each month. The "January Thaw" was unusually mild. A few days reach the low sixties. I was worried that this would bring on sickness with the extreme temperature changes. Our efforts at disinfecting the cell houses and Chief Steward Towne's efforts in the kitchen were successful. We quietly passed into spring. With the exception of the overcrowded conditions, the prisoners and staff were healthy and content with the changes that the General had made last year.

I found out from the March 21st 1897 Providence Journal, that the boxing match held on March 17th in Carson City Nevada American Champ Jim Corbett knocked out British Boxer Bob Fitzsimmons in the 14th round. I'm not looking forward to seeing the Boss today. He takes great joy in taunting me about my being British and how the Americans seem to keep winning over the Brits. It is all in good fun. I've been looking into becoming a citizen of this nation. I don't know how my mother and father would react to my giving up my British citizenship. But I have no intention of returning to England except for maybe a visit to Mum and Dad.

Early summer things began to change. I had a kitchen worker report to sick call complaining of constipation, fatigue and headache. He had a rash on his abdomen that was distended. I had him moved into the ward of the infirmary. My suspicion that it maybe typhoid fever. My suspicions proved correct. The condition spread to another prisoner who worked in the kitchen. And then an inmate who worked the farm. I knew we were in trouble when I had a staff member come to me with the same symptoms.

The prison was in the throes of a full epidemic of typhoid fever. Thirteen of the best of the prison personnel to include the Deputy Warden and Chief Clerk were sent to city hospital. The remaining personnel took their chances at the prison hospital among the prisoners. There were a total of thirty-six prisoners infected.

The Warden and I met with Dr. Keene in an attempt to find the source of the epidemic. One cause could be the practice of using human waste to fertilize the fields. Early harvest of lettuce and tomatoes were eaten without being cooked. The General stopped this practice immediately and plowed the crop under. Cooking of other farm items was required to kill the bacteria.

Another suspect was the water system may have become contaminated. The resources of the State Hospital at Howard was used to test all of the wells at the institutions, resulting in new piping being placed and one of the old wells being closed. No final conclusion was reached on the cause of the epidemic but the results were devastating for the staff.

Only seven of the thirteen staff that were sent to city hospital came back alive. Among the survivors were Frank Viall and Ed Slocum. Of the thirty-six prisoners, all recovered but one aged man.

The epidemic did bring about some positive changes to the prison. The installation of cot beds in place of the tall iron bedsteads and hard-packed, high, straw mattresses took place. After I had reported to the Warden that the men that were delirious from fever often fell to the floor and injured. The Boss not missing an opportunity began making mattresses from cotton batting. Over a period of two years had replaced all the mattresses at the prison with the new cotton batting type. He then proceeded to sell them to the psychiatric hospital, raising the funds that covered the cost of providing them to the prison. The old mattresses were burned under my supervision, to prevent any spread of diseases. The prison slowly returned to normal. It took some time to train and replace the six staff lost to typhoid.

I was recognized by the Warden for my efforts during the epidemic. A copy of a letter of commendation was read at all the prison roll calls. A copy was sent to the Board of Charity and Corrections and placed in my personnel file. I also received a small increase in salary. I sent a copy to my parents in England, not to brag. It was God's work, "God moves in a mysterious way His wonders to perform". The unfortunate typhoid epidemic, disastrous to the prison personnel, was an entering wedge for better things for the prison population.

The following year the prison was equipped with electric lights. For years, the electric light line ran by the front of the prison and could have been cut into the prison at any time. But because of politics and those who did not want to appear to be soft on criminals, this modern aid was not accorded us. The first case of appendicitis ever operated upon in the prison hospital I did by the aid of candles and a dimly burning lantern that was held by interested prisoners in the prison hospital ward. Following this surgery I met with the Warden to enlist his help to get the Board and Representatives and the State Legislature to fund the cost of installation. The Boss impressed upon them how modern lighting would enhance security and allow for longer work hours during the winter for prisoners thus improving production. The vote in the Legislature was close but passed. At the same time money was authorized to add modern toilets to all the cells, eliminating the slops buckets. The Boss and staff were happy to see the slops buckets eliminated. They were always a problem with some prisoners throwing the contents at staff. Also, the Warden had no use for the contents on the fields following the epidemic.

Changes came slowly. The acceptance of "Women Visitors" came slowly. These women were the forerunners of the social worker. They were not looked upon well by most of the staff. The Boss had no use for them. He felt that they made the prisoners discontented, and aroused sexual interest through their sympathy for the underdog and views that the prisoners were falsely imprisoned etc. Their actions also extended into intrigues with and by outsiders striving to get pardons for the prisoners. The General felt that the Chaplin's teaching and visitation to prisoners were sufficient for the redemption of the prisoner if he earnestly desired to repent of his crimes. I had to admit that they gave me some concerns also. On several occasions, my treatment of some of the prisoners medical conditions were questioned because, "my treatment was not what their doctors would have prescribed".

There was one occasion that one of these women was discovered bringing contraband into the facility. When the inmate was found with the contraband he quickly informed Deputy Slocum where he had gotten it. And willingly participated in a plan to work with the Deputy to catch her in the act of smuggling items to him. She was shocked that he had done so, "I love you and I thought that you loved me, that's why I did what I did". That excuse didn't hold much water with the Boss. She was charged with the crime and placed at the Women's Work House. One change that was brought about by this incident was the training of all non-custody people coming into the facility to work. The training was conducted by The Deputy, Reverend Nutting, and myself.

It appears to me, that there is a great field for service to God and the State in the redemption of prisoners by the ministers and priests who service the Institutions. Men should be trained for the purpose of dealing with prisoners, the causes of their downfall and what brings them to their ruin. I believe, from my experience, that along with Institutional Chaplains, there should be men trained to be fit to deal with this area of Social Service. Not all Ministers and Priests are meant to be Chaplain, just as not every physician can become a useful prison doctor. But with training and experience, they can become a positive disturbance to a well-ordered regime, and bring about positive changes in the future.

CHAPTER 11

STRUGGLE ON
TWO FRONTS

I made plans to go to Boston on the train with Bill McCaw. September 1ˢᵗ the city just opened its new underground subway, and we wanted to experience the new system. Boston is a wonderful city to visit. There are many fine restaurants, especially Italian ones in the northern part of the city. While we were in the city we attended a political rally for William McKinley the Republican candidate. He is running for President of the United States against William Jennings Bryan. I do find American politics fascinating.

The winter of 1898 was harsh. Here in New England we are accustomed to bad winters but this year the southern part of the United State was hit hard. All the southern states were hit hard with snow. For the first time in anyone's memory snow from northern

Florida to South Carolina was measured in feet not inches. The poor people living in those states were not prepared for a winter such as this. Many died of exposure. President McKinley declared a state of emergency throughout the south. The lack of winter clothing and home heating had citizens moving into public building. Rhode Island's Governor had organized a collection of winter clothing to send down south to help with the emergency. The poor were affected the most as with most disasters. The Prison and jail, fared well over the winter. A new heating system was in place piping steam from the main power plant. We also remained connected to our own system as a backup. Other than some cases of minor frost bite and the regular cases of the common cold, the prisoners and I had an uneventful winter season.

On Wednesday morning of February 16th, I picked up my copy of the Journal and across the front page the headline read "USS MAINE SANK IN HAVANA HARBOR". I went on to read that sabotage is suspected. I arrived at the prison and stopped in the Warden's Office. I asked if he had seen the morning paper. "I did. If this turns out to be sabotage, we will be involved in another war, Henry." I told him I didn't think that Spain would be so brazen as to sink a United State war ship. "I don't know, Doctor, something like this didn't have to be approved back in Spain. A local big shot could have had too much to drink and got stupid, wanting to make a name for himself. We will have to see where this is going." I bid the General a good day and proceeded to the infirmary to start my day.

Following the medication line one of the prisoners, assigned to the infirmary as a janitor, called me over and began telling me about an incident of an escape attempt that took place Sunday evening. "Jack Willard got an awful pounding. He was cut on the head and it wasn't dressed and was filled with pus. It was all right to give him the works, but he should have a doctor look at him."

After lunch, I went to see the Deputy Warden. At the risk of being an outcast, I insisted on seeing the prisoner. He was a real bad actor, a killer, who had come back east from out west to escape being hung in Oklahoma. The Deputy asked if I knew what he had done. When I told him no he told me of what had taken place on Sunday evening.

"Well Doctor let me tell you what happened. Willard had fashioned a revolver out of wood, he then covered it with tin foil. On Sunday evening he met the officer alone in an obscure area of the cell house, and pulled the gun on him. He told him to put up his hands and tried to take Officer Henry's pistol. Tom had worked as an attendant in the hospital for the insane and had been trained to never strike a patient, but to wrestle him and subdue him not to injure him. Well, Tom dove into Willard trying to wrestle what he thought was a revolver from him. Tom's revolver fell from its holster to the ground and Willard and Officer

Henry struggled to gain control of the gun. No one heard the struggle and they both were a pretty even match. Tom was fighting to save his life and Willard was fighting to take it. Tom was able to kick it further away just as another prisoner came around the corner. Tom called to him to get the gun and get help. The prisoner obeyed and that ended the struggle. Officers arrived on the scene and in the process of taking Willard into custody banged him up a little." I asked how Officer Henry was doing. The Deputy told me he was fine just a few scrapes and bruises. I told him I understand, but I still need to see him to tend to his injuries. What's done is done, now I need to check him out. The Deputy and the hall officer escorted me to the "Dark Cells" underneath the floor in the center of the main prison. They opened the one containing Willard.

He was in the back corner of the small cell. I looked in, and had him come to the door so I could get a look at him. In the dim lantern light I could see his eye was swollen shut and a gash on the top of his head, most likely from a blow from a sap (blackjack) carried by the guards. I had him bend forward so I could examine the wound. Most of the gash was covered by hair matted in dried blood. When I completed my examination, we returned to the Deputy Slocum's office. I told him I would need for Willard to be brought to the infirmary for treatment.

"Doctor you will need to see the Boss about that. I don't have the authority to remove him, nor do I have the inclination to do so. He is a very dangerous prisoner, and a threat to the staff including yourself." I told Ed that I would see the Boss about the situation, and thanked him for taking me to check him out.

I went straight away to the Warden's Office. I arrived and knocked on his door. I was not an infrequent visitor to his office. I smile when I think of how intimidated I was when I first arrived at that door five years earlier. The Boss called from within for me to enter. He was seated at his desk in his shirtsleeves, pen in hand. When he saw me he stood and took his suit jacket from the hook and put it on. "Doctor, two visits in one day. To what do I owe this second visit? More news on the Cuban situation?" I told him no, the evening paper had not come out yet. That I was here to speak to him about prisoner Willard. I told him I had just checked on him in the solitary confinement cell and he needs medical attention. The Deputy said I needed to talk to you, in order to have him taken to the infirmary. "Do you know what he did to be put down there?" I told him I was told what happen and that Officer Henry was a fortunate man to have come away from this with his life. Also, Ed told me he was a little banged up but was doing fine and back on duty.

I told him that he had received a heavy beating when others arrived on the scene of the event. And, that I found a deep scalp wounds that were infected. Dirt and matted hair prevented me from treating him. Also, he was almost too lame to move to the door of the cell from the beating. "I'm not saying he didn't deserve it by no means. However at this point he does need treatment even though he brought the injuries upon himself by attacking a member of your staff." The General stood and walked to the window and looked out in silence.

The silence was broken when he asked me what I proposed. "Warden, I know he is a most dangerous prisoner. Had he reached the officer's pistol, he would have shot him instantly, and others as well. I know his record from other situations, yet I feel that the State would not tolerate cruel treatment of the wounded prisoner. This situation would not be to the credit of the Board and to you as Warden, if the story of such cruelty should break out in the public press."

The Boss quickly turned towards me. "Are you telling me that you plan to report this to the Board or the press?" I didn't flinch at his raised voice, and told him, "No I wouldn't do that. But that don't mean that it wouldn't get out through the prisoner grapevine or something mentioned by a visitor."

"Just what is it you want to do, Doctor?" I insisted that the prisoner be restrained in the Infirmary ward so that it would be impossible for him to escape. If he attempted to escape, I would put him under such chemical restraint that he would be oblivious to his surroundings until his wounds were healed. "You win Doctor. I want to talk to Tom Henry to give him a heads up on what is going on. He is on duty today and his going along with what we are doing will go a long way with the rest of the staff and how they will react to moving him out of solitary confinement. This event has made him a big man with the staff and even with the prisoners. In this line of work, Doctor, your reputation as being able to handle yourself goes a long way." I told him that also your reputation for being fair and compassionate also goes a long way, also. From what I hear, the prisoners themselves feel that the guy had it coming to him, but would be quick to resent what they thought of as abuse and cruelty. "Alright, Doctor, I will have the Deputy move Willard to the infirmary and secure him there. He should be there in about an hour or so." I thanked the Boss and took my leave, returning to the infirmary to await my patient's transfer. At times I feel as if I am fighting a battle on two fronts. The General and his staff and the inmates. It is a difficult chore to maintain a balance. It is important to the job I do here to remain impartial and treat my patients whether they be staff or inmates. I do think the Boss understands because he fights a tougher battle when you add the political climate into the mix. He serves at the pleasure of the Governor and needs the legislature's good will for prison funds.

True to his word, the prisoner was escorted to the infirmary by three guards. I was surprised to see that one of the escorts was Tom Henry. They placed Willard on one of the beds in the ward, and proceeded to shackle him hand and foot to the bed frame. Two of the guards left but Officer Henry remained. Henry and the inmate were having a conversation. I couldn't quite hear what was being said, but it wasn't loud and did not sound threatening to either person. I walked to the bedside to clean and inspect my patient's wounds. "I was never so surprised in my life when you jumped me," Willard was telling the Officer. "Out west, if I were holding a pistol on a guy, his hands would have gone up pretty damned quick." The prisoner's voice became louder. He wanted the other prisoners and staff in the infirmary to hear what he was saying. "I have to admit, Mr. Henry, you are one tough son of a bitch and got a set of balls, to have jumped me while I had a gun on you." Officer Henry took Willard's hand and they shook hands. It was done. What happens in prison stays in prison.

I cleaned and bandaged Willard's head wounds, checked him over for any other serious injuries. He just had scrapes and bruises. His ribs were sore, most likely from being kicked, but there were no broken bones. Had he been treated right after he was beaten down, I would have stitched up his head wounds. However it had been too long since the injuries to be stitched. He will wind up with some good scars when he is healed. When I told him, he laughed and told me that the scars would be the subject of some good stories.

The next day, while I was changing his bandages, he said to me, "Doctor, it was worth all I suffered to get to the hospital and get nice bread and butter and all the milk you can drink." He asked if he could get the shackles off. I told him that they will only come off when the Boss says they can come off, and I wasn't about to wear out my welcome at the Warden's office on his behalf again. "I'll not ask you to have these off again. I want to know I'm at least alive, and am great full to you for rescuing me from solitary." I informed him that it wouldn't have happened without Mr. Henry agreeing to you being moved. "I thought as much. He's a good man and has a reputation with the prisoners as being a fair guy." I smiled at Willard. I told him that now he also has a reputation for being a tough son of a bitch also. We both laughed. Upon leaving the infirmary the prisoner found he could put his life in better order. He became so much more cooperative that he was accorded a pardon and left the state for the West Coast.

By April, following the sinking of the Maine, we were at War with Spain. The Journal was full of reports on the war. The General was called upon by the Governor Dyer to assist in the training of the 1st Rhode Island Infantry for activation in the War. Who would have thought that at seventy one years old the Boss would be called upon to assist in training troops for war? His reputation and presence were enough to inspire the young troops of his first command he served as Lieutenant. His appearance on horseback clad in his Civil War uniform as he inspected the young soldiers preparing to meet the enemy on foreign soil, was something to behold. The first Rhode Island never saw combat in the war with Spain. They served in garrison in South Carolina. By December the war ended with the signing of the Treaty of Paris. Spain gave up the Philippines, Puerto Rico and Guam.

CHAPTER 12

TAKE CHARGE
OF YOUR LIFE

In late 1899 I received a cable from my sister back in England. My father had passed away. My mother was now living with my sister and her family. It came as quite a shock to me. The news left me saddened that I had not been able to return to England for a visit since I had left almost ten years ago. I have given a great deal of thought of returning to England for a visit, but had never followed through. I conversed with my family about returning. However they encouraged me to remain in the States and pursue my life and career in America.

I continued with my normal routine the day I received the cable but my mind was not on my work. It was on my family in England. My mother was not a well women. She has asthma, and has suffered from breathing problems since I was a child. I am grateful that my sister and her husband are able to take her in. After my rounds I plan to go to Providence and send a cable to my sister expressing my appreciation for all she is doing. I do feel guilty about leaving her to care for mom. Life has a way of surprising you. I always thought that mom would pass away before dad. And that I would be there for them.

The Boss has a staff meeting scheduled for three o'clock in the afternoon, Tuesday the 5th of December. I love the General's staff meetings. He talks and we listen. Then we talk to each other and figure out how to accomplish what he just told us. I have found that my efforts at reform within the prison is better served by a one on one with the Warden. Putting him on the spot in front of the command staff would not work in making changes in how things have been done here for thirty years. All so the changes gets to be his ideas. If it became general knowledge that I was trying to interfere with operations of the prison, no changes would happen. If opposition wasn't from the staff it would be a political push from the legislature.

We all arrived at the Boss's office and those who fit sat around the large table in the room. It was a custom that the higher the rank the closer to the Warden's desk you sat. I always opted for a seat in the corner of the room. I remember the Bible parable that said "It is better to be asked to move up than to be moved down to a lower seat by the master".

We all stood when the Boss arrived. "Please take your seats, gentlemen. I have a change to make on how the staff meetings will be conducted. As you know I have been very busy as of late, in Providence with budget hearings. There is also a move afoot to replace me as Warden. Some of my opponents in the legislature have been making comments about my age and the fact that I have been in office now for thirty one years. I think that it gets under their skin that I have been Warden longer than some of them have been born." We all laughed. I know he has been the Boss longer than I have been alive. "We will be starting each staff meeting by each of you giving a one or two minute report on what has been happening in your area of our operation, and what is the biggest problem you are having in accomplishing your duties." I felt sorry for a few of the men. They were not expecting to have to speak and had a problem communicating their views. When it was my turn, I knew that I had to be careful with what I brought up. I mentioned that I suspected that contraband was coming into the prison in the form of drugs. My concern was not only those I should have being the prison physician, but it also indicated to the custody staff that I was also concerned with the security of the facility. The reason my suspicions were aroused was, that new prisoners who were addicted to drug were not exhibiting any symptoms of withdrawal from the substance. That was an indication that they were still able to obtain enough drugs to ward off the discomfort of abstaining from the use of the substance. I informed Day Supervisor that I was told during a conversation with one of the prisoners I was treating that one inmate in particular had received drugs through the mail. The Captain spoke up that all of the prisoner's mail had been checked and nothing was found. At the end of the meeting the Boss asked that I remain after the meeting. As the meeting broke up some staff gathered in small groups and discussed things that were brought up. I was speaking with Deputy Slocum on what I had mentioned about drugs coming in the mail. I told him my source of information was an inmate who had been inside for many years and had good information on the goings on in the prison. He asked who he was. I told the Deputy that I couldn't share who it was but that I believed what he told me.

After everyone had left the office. "Henry, please have a seat." I took a seat at the side of the Boss's desk, as he hung up his suit jacket. "Henry, I notices that you seem a little out of sorts today. And during the meeting you were dreaming out the window on occasion. Is there a problem that I should be concerned about?" I was a little embarrassed that he had picked up on my distraction. I told the Boss, no that I was fine, that I just had a few things on my mind. "Anything I can do for you, man? I don't want to pry, but you know that you can always come to me with anything that may be bothering you." I looked up into his face that reflected real concern for me. I could feel my eyes watering.

I looked away embarrassed by my show of emotion. "What is wrong, Henry?" That is when I came out with it, and told the General about the cable I had received informing me of the death of my father, and that my mother was now living with my sister and her husband.

"Oh, I am terribly sorry for your loss, Henry. I don't remember much about my father. He passed away when I was very young, and my family was not what you would call close." I told him that my mother was not a well woman and I was worried about her. My sister and her husband are wonderful people and will take good care of her. I just feel some guilt that I was not there for them. "Henry, I can approve a three month leave of absence for you, if you would like to sail back home to see your family. It will be with pay of course, I am sure that the Board will approve it. You have been such an asset to us here at the prison. I know Bill McCaw will fill in while you are gone." I thanked him for his offer, but I told him that my family feels that I need to stay in the States and pursue my own life and career.

"Well, lad, I am approving three days off with pay. A bereavement period that all staff receive that have lost a close family member." I thanked him for his concern, but I would be fine I told him. "Doctor, I didn't offer three days, I ordered three days. That is my prescription to our fine physician. Now just take your medicine and get better. I don't need a doctor in the prison with his head up his ass." We smiled and shook hands, and thanked him again.

On my way back into the prison I stopped at the Deputy's office. I knocked and entered. Ed was sitting at his desk with a pile of letters on the desk. He was examining the letters and envelopes, and the content of the letters. They were all encouraging letters, telling him to "be brave and grin and bear it". "Doctor what do you see here?" The Deputy spread the letters over his desk. I looked at them and picked a few up examining them. I told him that I didn't see anything unusual. "OK, Doctor, what don't you see?" I looked at him with a questioning look. "What don't each of these letters have?" I looked again closer. Again seeing nothing unusual. "Stamps man, stamps, there are no stamps on any of the letters. They have all been removed. I'll bet you my week's pay the stamps had "snow" under them. Just enough to keep him from getting sick. I've seen a lot of ways prisoners have tried to conceal drugs, in some instances, peanuts were found split at one end by a thin knife and held open the drugs would be dusted into the nut. When the knife is withdrawn, there was spring in the shell to close the crevice tight enough not to be noticed. This is a new one, I will have the mail officer remove all stamps from incoming letters as part of the review process. Thank your contact, Henry he was right on the money. You may begin to notice some prisoners getting a little drug sick in a few days."

The Boss was right, he usually is, and I did need the three days off. I didn't stay in my apartment while I was off on leave. I stayed in the city at the Westminster Hotel for two nights. I paid up to stay there. It cost me three dollars. Bill had offered me to stay with him or at his men's club in Pawtucket as his guest. I didn't want to put him out and I felt I needed some time alone to think about where my life was going. Even though my family recommended that I stay in the states, I was having some second thoughts. Should I go back to England with family or remain in Rhode Island. Bill and I made reservations for Thursday evening at the T.K. Club for dinner. I never did join the club, I always thought it was too far from Cranston to justify the cost of membership. Doctor McCaw has been a member for many years as was his father and uncle, and I was always welcome as his guest.

We road to Pawtucket in Bill's carriage. It was a cool evening ride, but I did enjoy getting together will him again. I thanked him for filling in for me during my three days off. When we arrived, we were greeted by name. I was surprised they had remembered me, but then again hospitality is their business. And Bill and his family are regulars.

The club was decorated for the Christmas season. We relaxed over drinks in the longue before going to our table. Bill expressed his condolences on the loss of my father, and asked after my mother and family. "Have you made any plans to return to England for a visit, Henry?" I told him that I had given it some thought, however my family said I should stay in the states and make my life here. "What do you think you should do? It is your life and you need to do what you think will be best". I told him that I actually was considering just going back to England and setting up my practice in Brighton where I was born. "Were you happy there, Henry?"

His question caused me to think. I noticed that my pause in answering made him a little uncomfortable. I told him I was sorry, but he did give an opportunity to think about my answer. "Well, Henry were you happy there? There must be a reason you traveled all the way to America to live and work." I thanked him, and told him his one question had taken a weight from my shoulders.

"You are a smart man Bill McCaw, and you have made me make a decision I have been fighting with myself over for several days. To answer your question Bill, I was not happy there in Brighton. I am the youngest of my siblings and was always the baby. Even after graduating from Medical School in Cambridge, I was the baby of the family. I needed to get away, I needed to be on my own, and that's what brought me to the States. I was thinking, that I could return to England and take care of my mother now that my father has passed away. However I know my mother and she would be the one taking care of me. I know that my sisters and my brother would grow to resent that, even though my intentions were honorable. I would always be viewed as the baby of the family." Bill was smiling from across the table. "You know, Bill? I think my family, especially my father, was proud of me and my decision to move to the States on my own. He and the whole family thought it took a great deal of courage to travel here not knowing anyone and making it on my own. I know they were proud to hear that I was hired as the first full time physician for the prison and working for the State of Rhode Island.

As we talked the waiter returned and asked if we were ready to order. Bill looked at me. "Yes I think I will have Dr. McCaw's favorite, the pork chops." Bill ordered a sirloin steak. We continued our conversation. "To tell the truth, Bill, I was thinking about becoming a citizen of your great country. The reason I haven't done anything about that has been my family, especially my father. I didn't know how he would feel about me giving up my citizenship in my home country. I think the time may be right to put aside any thoughts of returning to England." Bill told me he thought it sounded like a good idea, but did caution me to give it a lot of thought. He also offered to sponsor my citizenship. I thanked him for his offer. "I will keep your offer in mind." Our dinner arrived and both dishes look fantastic, as always. The pork chops had to be an inch and a half thick, served with roasted potatoes and beets. Bill's steak was of equal size with mashed potatoes and butternut squash. When we had finished we returned to the longue for an after dinner drink to brace us against the cold ride back to Providence.

Bill dropped me off at the hotel and I went to my room. I would be returning to Howard tomorrow afternoon on the train. I spent the evening thinking over what my decision would be for my future. Many memories came to mind of my growing up in Brighton. Family and friends, as time passed, many had moved away. I thought of my mother, sister and brother. My brother and I had some problems between us. He always thought I was spoiled by my parents. He had to go to work after primary school, and I went to University. He always told me that I was my parent's favorite, he was right, I was. But I wouldn't admit it to him, and neither would they. But it was obvious to everyone in the family. My sister married at nineteen into a family of professional merchants with holdings throughout the empire. She and her husband never had children. Their home reflected her husband's status in business. They have plenty of room for my mother and I know will make sure she is well cared for. They also have domestic help to assist them. I sat at the desk in the room and began composing what I wanted to cable them.

"My dear Sister Gwen,

I was quite shocked to receive your cable of Father passing away. I pray he did not suffer and passed with family about him. I am quite grateful that you have taken Mother to live with you and Alfred. I know she is in good hands. I do feel I should return to Brighton and help where I can, but I do agree with you that my life should be here in America now. Please share this cable with Brother Douglas and give him my best. Father had told me how well he was doing at Scotland Yard. He mentioned that he was up for Chief Inspector. I hope the position came through for him. He always was a good law officer. I often smile when I think of him and his duties arresting criminals and I am here in the States caring for them. I will end now and write you a post in a few days. I have much to tell you that will not fit in this cable. Sincerely yours, Brother Henry."

In the morning I will take the cable to the telegraph office. I went down to the hotel bar, in the lobby, for a night cap. I was still upset about my Father and my not being there for the family at a time like this. I sat alone at the bar thinking about my childhood and life in Brighton. A man sat down beside me. I didn't look at him just gave him a little extra room when he took his seat. After a few minutes he said, "good evening Doctor". I looked up into his face. He looked familiar but I couldn't place where I had met him. I bid him hello. He could tell that I was searching my memory for where I had met him. "You don't remember me do you, Doctor." I begged his pardon, and told him his face was familiar however I couldn't place where I knew him from. "Johnathan, Doctor, your man from Brooks Brothers." Now I remember. I hadn't seen him face to face in quite some time. I have been ordering what I needed through the concierge program. I apologized and told him it has been quite some time since we had been together. "Yes. I hope my selections that I have made for you were all satisfactory." I assured him that they were. "I thank you for your confidence and your business. As you know part of my salary is commissions on my sales and good customers as yourself, Doctor, helps support me and the family." He shook my hand. "Let me buy you a drink, Doctor." I thanked him but declined, telling him I had a few things to take care of in my room.

"Johnathan, I do have a favor to ask of you. I know you are off work for the evening, but if you could pick me out a new overcoat. My overcoat has become a little shabby, and I have discovered a moth hole under the arm, it really should be replaced." He inquired on a color. "Black will be fine it will go with all my suits." Johnathan told me about something new that has just came in for this winter. It is an overcoat that has a button out lining that will allow it to be worn from fall into early spring also in rain and snow. "I think that would take care of me just fine. When you can box it up and sent it to my residence." He did caution me that this style of coat is a little costly. "Johnathan, my friend I am sure it will be fine. An overcoat like you described will be a savings in the course of the year." He thanked me for the order and offered to take me to the store this very evening. He told me he would open up for me and provide me with the overcoat today. "No, no, thank you. This is your time, good man. Finish up your drink and go enjoy dinner with your family. I will be going to my room. It was nice seeing you again. My next time in the city I will stop in to see you."

I left the hotel bar and walked down the street to Haven Brothers for a bite to eat. When the city I always enjoy stopping at Haven Brothers. It opened about ten or twelve years ago. When I was living in Providence, I would go for a late dinner. What made it so unusual is that it was a restaurant on wheels. Every day it was pulled into place about 6:00am and be taken away around 11:00 pm. The food was a simple fare but well prepared and prices right. I had a roast beef sandwich with cheese.

I needed both hands to eat, and washed it down with a nice cup of coffee. I was set for the evening.

On the way back to the hotel, I thought about my life in Rhode Island and the friends that I have made since living here. I have made a good life in America. I have been a much happier man here than in Brighton. For being a foreigner, I have been accepted and befriended by many of the people I have met. The General not the least. He has treated me well, even though we have been at odds on some of the conditions at the prison. Our discussions have always been professional. I recalled one time it did get quite heated, and he asked me to leave his office. The next day when I ran into him on the way into the building. He wished me a, "good morning, Henry, and how are you today, Doctor?" I responded that I was well. I did start to apologize for my actions the day before.

He interrupted me and told me, "Henry, that was

just business. We will not always agree on policies and operations of the prison. That is just business. You are a fine man my friend. I do need your input on my decisions, and I do value your work here. New Ideas coming into existence is like giving birth. Change doesn't come without pain, it is the end results that counts. I know that I can be stubborn. But I do try to keep an open mind. I have been Warden for over thirty years and have problems making changes to things that have worked well. Keep up the good work, Doctor. We do seem to work well together." We shook hands and I went to my work in the infirmary.

I spent the night in the hotel giving a lot of thought about my life. What my future would be and what I wanted it to be. I came to the conclusion quickly that my life was here in America. I had a good career as the Prison Physician and there is room for advancement within the State Hospital System. Bill had even asked if I would like to be his partner in private practice. I jokingly told him that I had a private practice that couldn't change doctors or move away. By morning my mind was made up. It was time for me to take charge of my life. It is my life to lead and I decided that I would remain in America, and at least, for the time being, remain as the Prison Physician. I packed up my valise and checked out of the Hotel. I began my walk to the Providence Train Depot. I reached the corner of Weybosset and Custom House Streets and there it was the Federal Custom House.

The flag of the nation was flying strong against the morning breeze. Without another thought I climbed the thirteen granite steps to the entrance and went inside. As the door closed behind me I saw a soldier in uniform and asked him where I could get the papers needed to become a United States Citizen. "Welcome to America." He said as he stretched out his hand towards me. I shook his hand and looked at my left hand holding my valise. "When did you arrive?" he asked. I smiled, still shaking his hand, and told him that I had been in America for several years and that I worked in Cranston. I didn't tell him where or that I was a Physician. I informed him that I had finally made up my mind that I would stay in the United States and not return to England. "Well good for you, Sir and welcome again." He directed me down the hall to the office of immigration.

I walked to the office and went inside. A gentleman in a gray suit looked me over, smiled and asked "Do you speak English?" I smiled and answered and that I do. "Well, I guess you do." He said with a chuckle, hearing my British accent. I told him I would like to become a citizen, and would like to get a copy of the requirements and any forms that may be required. He walked to a file cabinet and took out several pieces of paper and a small booklet of information. "Here you go." He handed me the material. "You will be needing a sponsor, and there will be a test you will need to take. Depending on the test the process will take a few months." I took the forms and booklet and thanked him. "Good luck, sir." I thanked him again and left the office. As I walked past the soldier at the door, I held up the papers and smiled. He nodded and held the door for me as I left. I folded the papers and put them and the booklet into the inside pocket of my top coat.

I was on time for the noon train to Howard Depot. On the ride to Cranston I looked over the booklet I was given. Much of the material I already knew. I found some of the history of America funny. It spoke of the relationship between England and the American Colonies, and the two wars with England. Now I was reading the rest of the story. History, after all, is written by the victor. But I did learn it with a different slant in Brighton Primary School.

The train pulled into Howard Depot. I gathered up my belongings and stepped down onto the platform. I almost bumped into Bill McCaw who was waiting for the train to return to Providence. "Henry! How are you doing? Ready to get back to your patients, I trust? Don't worry not much to report. I had a quiet few days filling in for you." I thanked him, and told him that it was relaxing few days and it gave me time to think about my life and future. I told him we would talk about my intentions. And, this time it would be my treat. I suggested that we take the train to North Kingston. I had heard of a place I wanted to try. The Carriage Inn and Saloon, I hear has excellent sea food. "It's a date. I have never been there myself, and I do like sea food." We bid our farewells and I started up the hill to the Residents Hall. I greeted those in the parlor and they expressed their sympathy for the loss of my father. I thanked them, and climbed the stairs to my apartment.

Several pieces of mail and notes were on the floor inside the door. They had been slipped under the door in my absence. I gathered them up and put them on the desk. I went into the bedroom and placed my valise on the bed and began to unpack. I took the citizenship forms and booklet from my overcoat pocket and hung the heavy coat up. I removed my suit coat and tie and sat to look over the letters and notes that had been left for me. Most of the notes were from staff of the prison, expressing their sympathies for the loss of my Father. A letter from my sister that was sent prior to my Father's death. There was no mention of his being sick. She would not want to worry me, if he was sick upon her writing the letter. There was also a lengthy note from the Boss, expressing his sympathies for my loss.

I sat at the desk and looking over the forms for applying for United States Citizenship. One of the glaring sections was about sponsorship. It required that I have a citizen of the United States willing to sponsor me to become a citizen. Several years ago Nelson had offered to sponsor me should I ever wish to become a citizen. I told him I appreciated the gesture, but I was not ready to do so at the time. I wondered if the offer was still available. Bill McCaw had also offered to do so over dinner at the T.K. Club, a few days ago.

I returned to work in the morning. Everyone was so kind in expressing sympathies for my loss. Even some of the prisoners told me that they had heard that my Father had passed away and that the Reverend had offered prayers for me and my family at church services on Sunday. During sick call the Warden came into the infirmary. The Guard called attention as he entered, and saluted. The Boss returned the customary salute and called "At ease". He took his regular seat to watch the sick call line. Following Sick call he and I went into the examination room and closed the door.

"How are you doing, Henry? Is there anything I can help you with? Do you need a few more days?" I thanked him for his concern and offer, and told him that I was doing fine. I also thanked him for the days off, telling him that I did need to think, and make plans for myself and my future. I told him that I had decided to remain in Rhode Island and put any idea of returning to England behind me. I informed him that if I were to return home in the future, it would only be for a visit and I would return to the States. The General raised the issue. "Remember, Henry, I did offer to sponsor your citizenship. That offer still stands. The Country, Rhode Island and the prison would all benefit having a citizen such as yourself." I thanked him for his comments and told him that I had stopped at the Customs House and picked up the forms and literature for citizenship. "Good for you man. The turn of the century is just around the corner. A perfect time for a new beginning.

By the way, I hope that you will join me for Christmas dinner again this year?" I said, I would be most happy to join him. "We will be getting together following church services. Just a small group, Frank and Alice, Ed and Mrs. Slocum, the Reverend Nutting and his wife. If you have a guest you would like to bring feel free to bring them along." I asked if I could bring anything for the get together. "No, No I have everything all arraigned. I have planned combining both Christmas and New Year's celebration this year. When I was young I never thought I would see a new century. Who would have thought I would see 1900. During my life, there were days I didn't think I would see the next morning." He gave out a chuckle. "Turned seventy two last month and still feel like I'm forty.

I have planned the usual for the staff also this year Ed will add a little more sweets to the sacks for the prisoners. I was also able to secure an additional $4.00 a month for the officers from the Board. They have not seen a wage increase for a few years. Also you and my command staff will be receiving an increase, starting in January." I thanked him for his work on everyone's behalf. "I haven't mentioned the pay raise to anyone, except Frank. He has to prepare the books to reflect the changes, you know. So I would appreciate you keeping this to yourself." I assured him I would. I smiled and told him what happens in my examination room stays in my examination room. We both laughed and the Boss bid his farewell and left the infirmary.

It was a cold walk from my apartment to the prison. There was still snow in patches along my regular route. The tower guard came out of his tower and called down to me as I passed wishing me a Merry Christmas. I waved and returned his greeting. "Merry Christmas and a Happy New Century!" He waved back and returned to the warmth of his post.

I was running late for Christmas services. I climb the steel stairs to the prison chapel, and knocked on the heave steel door. It swung open and the guard gestured me through the door. Reverend Nutting was just starting the service. He saw me enter and waited until I took my seat in the same row as the Boss and the Deputy. Following the Christmas service the Warden stood and took the stage. He wished all those present a Merry Christmas and a Happy New Year. He made note that we were beginning a new century. "Next week will usher in the 1900's. I have been planning a special celebration for everyone for New Years. I understand that Prison is not where you men like to spend your New Years. However I hope that you will take this as an opportunity to pledge to make changes in your lives and start a fresh. Later this evening there will be some sugary treats distributed for Christmas. I hope you enjoy them." The General then shook hands with the Reverend and walked off the stage. He and the rest of the guests proceeded to leave the chapel. I stayed behind to wish the officers and some of the prisoners a good Christmas and New Year. I then made my way down the stairs and out the front door to the Warden's Residence.

I arrived at the front door, and knocked. I could hear joyous laughter coming from inside. Following a stronger knock the door opened. Filling the doorway was the Warden.

"Welcome, Merry Christmas! Henry, Merry Christmas." I returned his greeting, and removed my overcoat, the Boss took it hanging it on one of the empty hooks to the left of the door. "Come in, I'm sure that you know everyone. Help yourself to some punch or eggnog, both will warm you up from your walk." The punch smelled of rum, the eggnog smelled of brandy. I chose the eggnog. Taking a sip it did warm me, from my stomach radiating through my body. I scanned the collection of people in the parlor. Ed Slocum and his wife Lucy, Frank and Alice Viall, Bill McCaw with a young lady I didn't recognize, The Reverend and Mrs. Nutting. Also Dr. Keene and his wife. Bill came over to me with the young lady on his arm. "Merry Christmas, Bill. And who is this young lady? We have never met."

"This is my niece, Victoria. Vickie, this is my friend Dr. Henry Jones the Prison Physician." She smiled and curtsied. I took her hand and kissed it.

"How nice to meet you Miss McCaw." She quickly corrected me. Telling me she is Victoria Kelley and to please call her Vickie.

Bill chimed in, "Sorry old man, I should have told you Vickie's last name. I didn't think." I assured him it was fine. "Vickie is visiting for the holidays. I picked her up at the Pawtucket Depot last evening. I was sure the General wouldn't mind if I brought a guest. Vickie lives in Braintree, just outside of Boston, with her mother and father. She will be moving to Providence soon. Vickie has finished her studies as a nurse and will be starting work at Rhode Island Hospital the first of the year. My sister and her husband asked me to show her around the city and assist in finding her a safe place to live close to the hospital."

"Well, I congratulate you Vickie. I trust you will make a wonderful nurse. May I get you some punch or eggnog?" She told me that that would be delightful. We walked together to the large bowls of libations. I scooped a cup of punch for her. Bill had left us to chat and was across the room speaking with Dr. Keene and his wife.

"I can tell that you are from England Doctor."

"Please call me Henry. Yes I was born and brought up in Brighton not far from London. I moved to the states some seven years ago. With the support of your uncle, I was able to secure a position with the State. At the present I am the Physician here at the prison."

"That must be a challenge, Henry, and I imagine it has some danger to it. Aren't you worried that you could be attacked by the prisoners? I would be terrified that a murderer or other ruffians would kill me or worse."

"Actually, I feel quite safe. There are guards that do

a wonderful job keeping order. Also I am viewed by the prisoners as being there to help them. I am the person who treats their illnesses and, if need be, patch them up after an altercation. Warden Viall has been a fine boss and friend. At times we do have our differences of opinion. But, we always seem to come to a compromise. He is a strong personality, with a very difficult job to do. The General has had quite a life. I admire him greatly."

"My uncle also speaks very highly about him."

As we were talking the Warden called out to everyone that, dinner has arrived and guided everyone into the dining room. Both Bill and I pulled out Vickie's chair. She thanked us and took her seat, with Bill on her left and myself on her right. The table was actually two long tables put together in order to fit all the guests. The Boss took his seat at the head of the table. Two inmates were serving as waiters dressed in crisp white kitchen uniforms. The Chief Steward arrived at the table carrying a large ham, placing it in front of the Warden along with a large fork and carving knife. The Reverend Nutting gave the blessing and the Warden began carving the ham. A finer Christmas Dinner I have never seen.

Following dinner we all went into the parlor. The Boss had some announcements to make.

"My friends, I hope all of you enjoyed your dinner. While I have all your attention. I would like to invite all of you to come back on New Year's afternoon for some entertainment that will take place in our chapel. I do not want to spoil the surprise, but I am sure you will be glad that you attended. This is a special New Year, being the beginning of a new century. I did not want to let the occasion pass without making it memorable for all of you and those who work and, unfortunately, call the prison home on this occasion. Also I have been informed that our new Governor, William Gregory will be re-appointing me as Warden and Keeper for the State Prison and the Providence County Jail, for another term." We all applauded the announcement.

"I do hope that you will be attending the show, Vickie? Should you need someone to escort you, it would be my honor." I was hoping she would be attending. I do wish to see her again. "I am looking forward to seeing you again, if you would like?"

"That would be nice, Henry. I have only my uncle here in Rhode Island and have not met many people. I will speak to Uncle Bill and see if he will be attending. If so he will bring me back to Howard for the entertainment."

The Warden walked over to Vickie and me. "Merry Christmas Miss Kelley, and also to you Henry. I trust that you will be attending the show on New Year's? I promise it will be a real treat."

"Why, yes Sir, we were just making plans to do so. And please Warden, call me Vickie. Thank you for a wonderful dinner. I know that you were not expecting Uncle Bill to bring me along."

"My dear, you are a delightful addition to our celebration. I am pleased that you attended. I imagine that our fine Doctor is pleased also." The Boss's comment caused me some embarrassment. I glanced at Vickie and saw a slight smile and a blush. As usual, the General was correct, I was most pleased to meet Vickie. He had great talent in reading people and their emotions. I was quite taken by her, and hoped that we would see more of each other. Bill made his way across the room, and joined us.

"Well Nelson, I see you have met my Niece. She will be starting work at the hospital in Providence the first week in January."

"That's wonderful, Bill. I hope to see more of her, she seem like a fine young lady, and is welcome anytime. I'm sure Dr. Jones agrees, don't you Henry?" The Boss raised his glass of punch to his lips and smiled behind the glass. I felt flushed.

"Yes, Yes I do Sir. I would very much enjoy seeing Miss. Kelley again." I took the Warden's teasing as an opportunity to convey my feelings to Vickie without being too forward. I looked at Vickie and she was smiling and so was her Uncle. I wondered, in my mind, if our meeting was not by chance, but a conspiracy between Bill and Nelson to bring Vickie and me together. I quickly put it out of my mind as pure fantasy. To my delight, Bill changed the subject.

"Well, my dear, I think we need to be leaving. It is a long ride back to the city and will be getting cold as the sun goes down. Thank you, Nelson for a wonderful dinner and get together. I will be seeing you on New Year's Day. My Niece will most likely be attending also."

"That's great. We will be looking forward to seeing you on New Year's."

The "We" was for my benefit, I am quite sure. Again I took the opportunity, supplied by the Boss, "I am looking forward to seeing you again, Vickie. I hope the week passes quickly."

"As do I, Henry. I am curious about what the Warden has planned, and of course seeing you again will also be nice."

I didn't quite know how that was meant. If I was just a happenstance of her attending the show, or if, she really was looking forward to seeing me. Bill and Vickie departed for Providence and I rejoined the guests.

The General came up to me with two cups of punch, handing me one. "Well, my man, Bill's niece is quite a young lady. You appeared to be quite taken by her, and she with you."

"She is lovely, Sir. I do look forward to seeing her again. However I don't know if the feeling is mutual on her part." The Boss took a sip of his punch, and disclosed.

"I was talking with her Uncle and he was quite happy that the two of you seemed to get along so well. He was concerned that she would find it difficult moving and working here in Rhode Island. With no friends and only him to keep her company. After all you know he is quite fond of you, Henry. I hope that I am not speaking out of turn. I have had a bit of punch and it has loosened my tongue."

He chuckled and his whole body shook. We both laughed, and changed the subject. I attempted to find out about the show that was planned. But, the Boss's tongue was not loose enough to divulge his secret.

About six o'clock trays of sandwiches and cake was brought into the dining room. The Warden told everyone to take a plate and help themselves. The conversations among the guests was upbeat and varied from work related to hopes for the new century that was approaching. Word had spread among the guests of my plans to remain in America and become a citizen. Everyone was very welcoming. By half eight, the party was winding down and the guests were beginning to leave. I thanked the Warden for his hospitality and complimented him on his generosity, and told him I would see him tomorrow at work.

The week was a short week that passed slowly. It would be a weekend of anticipation. I was looking forward to seeing Vickie again on Tuesday, New Year's Day. A new year, a new century, and hopefully a new friend, maybe a new love.

Monday was New Year's Eve. I left work early. I had made plans with Bill to meet him and Vickie in Providence for the celebration of the new century. There were going to be fireworks over the river and a band concert at the State House. The new State House was still under construction. They had started building the new building in 95 and it was scheduled to be completed for the new century January 1900. But as usual with large projects it was running behind schedule. The new Governor still planned to have a celebration at the new location. Governor Gregory was set on completing the new building during his term.

I met Bill and Vickie at the Providence Train Depot. As the train pulled into the station I could see Vickie and her Uncle waiting on the platform. My heart began to race at the sight of her. Vickie and Bill walked to greet me. She reached out her hands to me and I took both her hands in mine. She pulled me to her and kissed me on the cheek. "Happy New Year, Henry. I am so glad you were able to come to celebrate with us." I thought my heart was going to jump out of my chest. I stuttered a response, that I was happy to see her again so soon. Bill broke our eye contact as he shook my hand and wished me a Happy New year.

We walked together from the depot up the hill to the new State House. Even with the scaffolding it looked beautiful. White marble dome in the center with a two story wing extending from each side. The wings were still under construction. The plan was to have the new State House open with the new century, however there were many delays. The old State house building on Benefit Street is still being used. It dates back to colonial times, it is a beautiful building but has become too small to accommodate current business. There must have been close to five hundred people already there waiting for the concert to begin. We found a spot to stand about fifty feet from the bandstand. It was cold but the large crowd blocked the wind and standing close to Vickie I didn't feel cold at all. We waited about twenty minutes and we received a welcoming speech from the new Governor. Following his remarks the band began to play.

The concert lasted about an hour or so. It ended as it began with the playing of "America". I smiled to myself because I recognized the tune. The words "My Country, Tis of Thee" was different but the tune was "God Save the Queen, the British National Anthem. It was quite entertaining when I disclosed this to Vickie by singing it as the band played on.

The sun had set and we made our way down the hill towards the Providence River to watch the fireworks display. We stood along the railing waiting for the show to begin. There were a number of vendors selling flags, noisemakers, and food. There was a cart selling hot chocolate. "Would you like some hot chocolate" I asked, Bill and Vickie. Both answered in the affirmative. And I made my way through the crowd, returning with the smoking cups of chocolaty delight. The cups were ceramic commemorating the New Year and new century. The show started with a thud, followed by an explosion of light and sparks high overhead. Several bursts followed one after another. Several were suspended in the air at the same time. The sound thundered through the city as if we were under attack, sound reverberating off the buildings. The ships in the harbor were silhouetted in the darkness by the explosions. This continued for about forty five minutes. Then there was silence. Hundreds of people and there seemed to be complete silence. About ten seconds of silence, that was replaced by cheers and applause from the crowd. In the excitement, Vickie turned and hugged me kissing my cheek, as I returned her embrace.

Bill offered to walk me back to the depot. But I told him I was fine and he and Vickie should head back home and get out of the cold. The last train stopping in Howard would not depart for an hour or so. I decided to hire one of the livery carriages to carry me back to my residence. Although it was cold the driver would get me back to Howard before the train would even leave the station. I didn't mind the additional cost. Attending the concert and seeing the fireworks display, not to mention being with Vickie for the evening, well justified the cost in my mind.

I went up to one of the liveries and before I could say a word, "Good evening Doctor", the driver called out. "Don't you recognize me, Doctor Jones?" I looked more carefully, as he pulled the scarf from around his face. I did recognize him it was my old landlady's Nephew Burt.

"Well if it isn't Burt. How are you doing old friend? It's been a long time." Burt chimed in with a quick calculation.

"Yep, it's been about seven years." I enquired about his Aunt and how she is doing. "She is getting along in age, Doctor. She is forgetting a lot lately and having trouble climbing the stairs to check the rooms. I have moved into the house to give her a hand keeping the place up."

"I didn't know that you drove livery, Burt" He said he added people to his freight service a couple of years ago. "Well, that is fine I wish you luck. Can you drive me back to my apartment in Cranston, Burt?"

"I sure can, Doctor. I'll give you my special family price, one dollar and twenty five cents." I didn't want to take advantage of him. After all it was New Year's Eve, and he surely would be busy tonight and it would take him an hour and three quarters to travel round trip to Howard.

"Burt I appreciate your gesture, but I don't want to take advantage of your good nature and friendship. How about we settle on Three Dollars." Burt thought for a few seconds and came back with two and a quarter? "Deal, two and a quarter it is, and thank you for the ride." I climbed up into the carriage. There in the seat was a heavy wool blanket, I wrapped myself in for the long cold ride to Cranston. Burt and I spent the ride talking about what he is doing and his Aunt. I caught him up on my work at the prison. I seemed like no time and he was pulling up the carriage in front of the Residence Hall. As I climb down from the seat, I palmed him his fair, shaking his hand at the same time. I gave him the three dollars that I wanted to give him in the first place. Before he noticed I was out of the carriage and walking to the door.

He waived and called out to me a "Thank You, and Happy New Year!" I waived back returning his good bye. HAPPY NEW YEAR AND HAPPY NEW CENTURY!!! January 1, 1900. I look for this to be a new beginning for me. An opportunity to take control of my life. I have made several New Year's resolutions. This year I will become a citizen of the United States of America. I will work harder at improving the lot of those patients and inmates that are being held at the State Institutions, and lastly I will try to expand my circle of friends beyond my work. Hopefully this will include, dear Vickie.

Following a hardy breakfast and coffee in the Resident Hall parlor with others who make this place home. I readied myself to attend the Boss's surprise entertainment at the prison. At noon I started out for my walk to the facility. It was a sunny early January day. The temperature was in the mid-thirties, with little wind. Following a brisk walk, I reached the entrance to the prison. I was greeted by several officers with New Year greetings. Deputy Slocum and his wife had just arrived, and we climb the iron stairs to the Chapel where the show would be taking place. I looked around the room to see if Bill and Vickie had arrived. "No they haven't arrived yet." Ed commented. He knew whom I was looking for. Most of the guests from the General's Christmas party were in attendance. Just before the inmates were to be allowed into the Chapel Dr. McCaw and his niece Vickie came through the door. I waved from them to come and sit next to me. I stood to greet them.

I stood and shook hands with Bill and took Vickie's hand and she leaned in and kissed my cheek. I looked at Bill and was sure I was blushing. Vickie took her seat next to me. "Last night was a wonderful New Year's Eve, wasn't it Henry?" I agreed and told her about my ride back to Cranston and about Burt.

The Guards began filing the prisoners into the Chapel and seating them row by rows behind the civilian guests. I recognized several Guards that were off duty but were attending with their wives to see what the General had arraigned for entertainment.

Once everyone had been seated, the room had muffled undertone of activity and conversations, until the Warden walked on to the stage. The Deputy Warden called the room to attention. All the prisoners and Staff stood. "At ease." The Boss called out, everyone took their seats. "I want to wish you all a Happy New Year and all the hopes and dreams for the new century, and welcome to our annual New Year afternoon's entertainment. This year will be very special. I was able to arrange a special show for all of you. Our performers today you will all recognize they are nationally known entertainers whom have agreed to come here today, free of charge, as a donation to our great State of Rhode Island. Let me introduce to you currently appearing at the Newport Playhouse, and Stars of Broadway, let us welcome RHODE

ISLAND'S FAVORITE SON AND HIS NEW BRIDE MR. AND MRS. GEORGE M. COHAN!!" The chapel erupted into cheers and applause that was defining. The Cohan's came running on to the stage hand in hand to the applause, and bowed. The Boss raised his hands to quiet the welcoming cheers.

"My Mother thanks you, my Father thanks you, my Sister thanks you and I thank you." His wife Ethel Levey at his side elbowed him. "Oh yes and my wife Ethel thanks you." The audience laughed and applauded. "Well Warden, this is the first captive audience I have ever had the pleasure of entertaining." Again cheers and laughter from the staff and prisoners. "A full house at the "Big House". The Warden told me I better give a good show or it's off to solitary for me." As the laughter continued the Warden shook hands with Cohan and Ethel and exited stage right. From stage Left another man appeared and took a seat at the piano. He began to play "God Bless America" and the Cohan's sang, encouraging everyone to join in. The show continued for an hour. Songs, many of which were written by Mr. Cohan, were sung by both entertainers. Ethel Levey, a star in her own right sang a selections of songs that were from many of the musicals she had appeared in on Broadway. The end of the show brought a standing ovation from everyone in the Chapel.

The Warden returned to the stage, still clapping. "Thank you Mr. and Mrs. Cohan. Thank you so much for coming here today. I want to thank your pianist also, what a great treat this was for every one of us."

"Then I take it, that you will give us the keys to get out of you prison?" The crowd again burst into laughter and applause. "Thank you, Warden for allowing us to come here today, and allowing us to leave." More laughter as they all shook hands, and left the stage.

The prisoners all filed out of the Chapel, with the guards escorting. The guests of the Warden all remained, commenting to each other how great the show was. After all the prisoners had left, the Boss and the entertainers came out from back stage, and down the steps. We all gave another round of applause to the Cohan's and their pianist. They all bowed. The General then introduced each of us to the Cohan's. It was quite a thrill for all of us.

Two weeks later, I filed the papers to become a citizen at the Custom House in Providence and began studying for my citizenship test. The Boss was very supportive and encouraging. I think he wanted me to score 100% on the test. After all he was to sponsor my citizenship and didn't want to be embarrassed. And, I didn't.

My New Year's resolution, to take charge of my life, and become a citizen of the United States of America, was accomplished on April 7, 1900. I was sworn in by the Honorable William P. Cross, United States Magistrate, in the court room of the Custom House. Present were Warden Nelson Viall, Dr. William McCaw, and my dear friend Victoria Kelley. I was very proud.

UNITED STATES OF AMERICA
DISTRICT OF RHODE ISLAND

CITY OF PROVIDENCE *April 7* 1 9 00

We do depose and say that we are citizens of the United States, that we have known *Henry A Jones* of *Cranston* who petitions to be admitted a citizen of the United States for five years last past; that he has resided in the United States for five years last past, and in the State of Rhode Island one year last past and during that time has behaved as a man of good moral character attached to the principles of the Constitution of the United States, and well disposed towards the good order and happiness of the same.

Sworn to before me

J Albert Millard
C H Dear

William P. Gross
Notary Public.

OATH OF ALLEGIANCE.

I do solemnly swear that I do absolutely and entirely renounce and abjure all allegiance and fidelity to any foreign prince, potentate, state or sovereignty—particularly to Victoria, Queen of the United Kingdom of Great Britain and Ireland.

whose subject I have heretofore been, and that I will support the Constitution of the United States of America.

April 7 1 9 00
Administered in open Court
Attest

Henry A. Jones

W P Gross

Clerk

DR. HENRY JONES
CITIZENSHIP PAPERS

CHAPTER 13
CHANGE COMES SLOWLY

I have written my family in England of my citizenship in the United States. I pray that they are happy for me. But it is my decision and I am truly excited and proud of the occasion. Decoration Day will be in a couple of weeks. I was surprised when the General asked me to accompany him on his annual mission to decorate the graves of those whom have fallen from his unit during the "Great War". He has gone alone ever since his Mary had passed away. I believe that he feels having me come an assist him is another part of his sponsoring my citizenship. Somewhat of a learning experience for me.

Decoration Day was a beautiful spring day sun shining and warm. The carriage was laden with flowers, as always, grown at the prison. Each of the graves we visited was with the same ritual, I laid the flowers, and the General stood at attention and saluted each headstone. The ritual was only broken at two graves, those of General Burnside and Ed's Father, Colonel John Slocum. At those graves, the General laid the flowers and knelt in prayer. With me helping him to his feet, he came to attention and gave a slow and deliberate salute. I did notice a tear in his eye, I looked away, as not to notice.

The spring and early summer of 1900 was a wonderful time. The prisoners were busy tending the fields and except for the occasional slight injury from their work most, were healthy. The prison staff were doing well enjoying the increase in their pay that went into effect last January. Vickie and I have been seeing each other every weekend since the New Year's show at the prison.

Independence Day (July 4th, 1900), Vickie and I celebrated by taking the street car from Providence to Crescent Park in Riverside. The Amusement Park was located at the end of the line in East Providence. It was, along with Rocky Point in Warwick, a major summer attraction. Both locations had beautiful carousels with hand carved horses, and shore dinner halls. We asked Bill if he wanted to join us, but he declined the invitation. I think both Vickie and I were happy he did.

It was a wonderful day, celebrating the independence of the United States from England. I almost felt like a trader to my country of birth. Not really, but Vickie kept teasing me all day, giving me history lessons on the American war for independence. Following enjoying the midway games and rides, we went to the shore dinner hall. We dined on clam cakes and chowder, and walked the boardwalk overlooking the bay.

The sun was setting when we began our return to Providence. I found it fascinating to watch the conductor switch over the cables on the street car. Being at the end of the line he was required to use a long hooked pole to flip the cable rig over for the return trip. The ride back to Providence seem short. Our conversation on the return trip was light. We spoke of our childhoods in Braintree and Brighton. There were many laughs. We got off the street car in front of the Outlet Company on Westminster Street. It was a beautiful summer evening so we walked to Vickie's apartment near the hospital. It was at her door that we had our first real kiss. She had always kissed me on the cheek before today. We said our goodbyes, and I walked back downtown. It seemed as if I was floating instead of walking.

I woke up in the morning, after a night of pleasant dreams. Again it was a beautiful Thursday morning. I readied myself for work and went to the cafeteria for breakfast. Following an egg, toast and a cup of tea, I headed to the prison along my usual route. Per as I do every morning, I waved to the tower guards as I passed the north wall. When I reached the carriage house, Charlie Brown was sitting in a chair repairing a leather harness. "Good morning Charlie, how are you this beautiful morning?" He looked up from his work.

He seemed troubled. "Is there something wrong? You look a little down."

"Oh, I'm sorry Doctor. I have a lot on my mind. Mister Frank, the clerk, informed me this morning that my sentence was almost served. I am being released on Monday the 9th." I congratulated him on his upcoming release, and asked why he was troubled by such good news.

"What's an old black man to do? I have no friends outside and no place to go, and no job. None of my family will take me in. I have been an embarrassment to them over many years. Everything and everyone I know is here. The General has been a good boss and treated me well, letting me tend to his horse and all."

I tried to console him, telling him everything will work itself out once he leaves. I reminded him that he would receive some money and a new suit upon his release. I assured him that he would be fine. "Thank you Doctor. I hope you are right. But I am scared to be outside all alone." He looked up from his work and had tears in his eyes. I patted him on the back, and told him I would be talking to him again before he was released. I had to report to the infirmary.

On my way to the infirmary I toured the housing units on my normal inspection. All was in order. It will get warm, as it always does in the cellblocks during the summer. Heat rises to the upper tiers of cells. The stone building stays fairly cool until the afternoon but then it works like an oven and holds the heat.

During the sick call line the Boss came into the infirmary. As the custom the officer call attention and the Warden took his usual seat as I continued to see the prisoners for a number of minor ailments. After the last prisoner, I asked him if we could have a talk in the office.

We closed the door. "I was talking to Charlie Brown this morning on the way in. Frank told him he was being released on Monday. His sentence has been completed." The Warden told me, that he knew that he was due to be released. "I've noticed that many of the long term prisoners have problems adjusting to life outside of prison." The General agreed that is a problem and that many of those released find themselves committing a crime to come back to prison.

"We had a prisoner, old George Webster, when he was released, we had to force him out of the prison. The poor old fella, kept trying to get back in every time we opened the door for hours. Finally he walked away and went into town. He went to one of the stores, threw a brick through the window, grabbed a bunch of stuff and sat on the curb and waited for the police to come and arrest him. You may remember him, Henry, he died here about five years ago." I did remember him, he worked in the print shop. "I'll miss "Old Charlie", he is a good worker and I've grown to like him over the years. Let me think for a while. Maybe I can come up with something to help him out. I have a lot of friends, maybe one of them will have something for him." I told the Boss that that would be a nice thing.

"Henry, I would like to meet with you on Monday in my office. There are a few ideas that I would like to talk to you about, and I think you are just the man to carry the ball on them. How is 10 o'clock? "Sick call will be done by then." I told him I would be there. The warden left to continue his morning rounds of the facility, and I returned to my duties.

At the end of the day, I started my walk back to my apartment. I could see Charlie sitting outside the carriage house smoking his pipe, deep in thought. I walked over to him, he stood to greet me. "Good afternoon, Doctor Sir, how was your day? I told him I was fine and I had a good day, except I was concerned about him and how he was fairing. "I feel like I'm losing my whole family but I have to make the best of what life I have."

I rested my arm on his shoulder, as he emptied his pipe. "You know, Sir, I brought all my troubles in life on myself. Starting when I was young, skipping school, and hanging out with all the wrong people. In my teens, I even ran numbers for the bookies all over the Negro section of Providence. I started boosting things from stores even before that. I've done a lot of bad things over the years. This last time I was sentenced for stabbing a white man I was trying to rob when he began to fight me. I got myself 30yrs to life this last bid." I asked him how old he was. "My last birthday I turned 62 I think." I'm not real sure about that though,

Doctor. No real good records were kept on birthing niggers before the war. But my mother told me that I was born a year after she came north from being a slave in the Carolinas. So we figured that be in '38 or so. That make me 62 this year."

Although I am not ignorant of American history, my conversation with Charlie was eye opening. He reached into his pocket and pulled out a cloth bag of "Bull Durham Tobacco" and stoked up his pipe, striking a match on the bottom of his boot. "I've been thinking Doctor. Maybe I can find some way to do some kind of work helping people to kind of make up for all the bad things I've done. I know, I don't have many years left, and if I do some good now the good Lord may be would forgive some of the bad I've done." I told Charlie that that sounded good to me and that maybe the Reverend Nutting could help out with that. "Yes Sir, he is a good man, I have had a few talks with him." I shook his hand, his head was in a cloud of tobacco smoke, as I bid him luck and I would stop to see him tomorrow before he was released on Monday.

The following morning, on my walk to the prison I didn't see Charlie as I usually did. So I just walked on by the carriage house and into the prison. I stopped at Frank Viall's office, he wasn't in, and so I crossed the hall and knocked on the Deputy's door, and entered. Ed was working on some reports. "Can I help you Doc?" I told him that I was looking for Frank. "He is up in the Boss's office working on something. I don't know what, but they have been getting together on something for a few days now." I thanked him and started my day with a tour of the Jail Wing.

At the end of the day, as I was leaving, I noticed a lot of activity at the carriage house. There was a pile of lumber stacked in front of the building. Being nosy, I walked over. I could smell pipe smoke so I knew that Charlie was around. "Charlie! Are you in there? I heard him call out. In a few minutes he came out, with his pipe clamped in his teeth. "What's going on?" I asked.

He was almost laughing as he told me. "Well, doctor, we are building me a room on the second floor. The General, fine man that he is, has offered me a job working for him. I can live here in the carriage house up stairs and do what I am doing now. The Boss asked me to stay. He knows he can trust me to do a good job and I thinks he likes having me around. It won't pay much. I won't be working for the State, he is paying me out of his pocket. But I don't need much and there is no rent and food is included." I have to admit that I was surprised on the news Charlie had. Even though I have a lot of respect for the General and I do like him. I never thought that he would do such a kind thing for an old prisoner. "He don't want me telling everyone what he did, but I know you will keep it under your hat. The Boss reminded me, "That what happens in prison stays in prison." I laughed, we both laughed, I told him that the Warden is always telling me that.

On Monday afternoon I went to the Warden's

office, for our meeting. I thought it was going to be about Charlie, I was prepared to tell him how happy I was to see what he had done for the old fellow. I knocked on the heavy oak door. And I was beckoned in. The Warden was standing in his shirt sleeves, his jacket and tie was hung on the hook. I knew that this was going to be a relaxed, unofficial meeting.

"Come in, come in, Henry." He was bent over a table with large plans rolled out over it. "I want to get your input on something I have been thinking about for some time. "As you know, we have a problem with young first time criminals coming into the prison and they are being exposed to hardened criminals and, so called, learning the trade. By the time they are released they are worse than when they arrived" I was nodding my head as he spoke. "I have been working on a way to separate the young first time prisoners from the older more hardened criminals. Working with Frank I have the numbers and it looks like we can house the first timers in the small cellblock. Ideally it would be nice to have a designated building and get them completely out of the prison, but one step at a time." I thought to myself if this was the same man I met some seven years ago.

"I am going to make a pitch in my budget to the legislature to add a teacher and a councilor to the staff. They would be primarily to work with the young guys. Henry, this is where you come into the plan. If you are willing to help promote this idea with Dr. Keene and the Board, and I will try to get some of my friends in the legislature to support it. Maybe between us we can do something with this problem. I have spoken to the Reverend about getting some volunteer help from the community. But, we do have to be cautious doing that. If something were to happen between them and a prisoner, the politicians and the press would blow the whole thing up, and we both would be out of a job." We continued to talk about the idea for about an hour or so. I told him I would do my best to promote the idea of a "Reformatory" as a part of the prison. "What a wonderful name for the program, Henry, a reformatory......to reform the young prisoners."

As I was about to leave I said, "Nelson that is a nice thing you are doing for Charlie, taking him on and all." The Boss stiffened at my comment."

"Nothing nice about it, Henry. You know that I don't do change well. I don't want to have to break a new prisoner in in caring for things at the carriage house. So don't go thinking I'm getting soft in my old age."

I smiled at him and shook his hand as I left. Wishing him a good rest of the day. And that I would give some more thought to the new "Reformatory".

Things had progressed on the Reformatory idea. The younger prisoners were now housed together. The legislature took the idea "Under advisement" but no money was allocated for a teacher or councilor. We were able to get a volunteer teacher, Jeff Cook, an older teacher from Cranston school. He volunteered to teach two evening a week. It was rumored that in his youth he was quite a ball player. He credited sports and the local police officer for keeping him out of jail.

The Reverend spoke to the Catholic Chaplin and got a Sister of Mercy to help out as a counselor. She was actually quite a good councilor. Definitely not a "Bleeding Heart". She is a Sister of Mercy an order that started in Ireland. They are definitely not faint of heart. Very unlike some of the other church ladies that volunteer at the prison, she is not one who coddles inmates feeling sorry for their being in prison. Her mantra was stand up and take responsibility for your actions and only you can change your life.

I had several planning meetings with the Boss on ways to accomplish the reformatory idea. The Warden always put me as the leading force behind the new programs. I understood that he needed to maintain his reputation of being a tough taskmaster both with the inmates and staff, but also in the eyes of the political powers in the Legislature. I had several meetings with the Board of Charity and Corrections on changes we were trying to bring to the prison and also for the State Institutions as a whole. Many of the conditions at the Institution for the insane were worse than at the prison. Very little real treatment of the feeble minded took place. The State was mostly just warehousing them. Keeping them out of sight of the "good citizens of the State".

I woke to the sound of the wind howling outside my window. It was a cold January 3rd 1901 morning. I dreaded my walk to the prison. I could see the cold wind whipping through the trees in the orchard behind the prison wall. After breakfast I bundled myself up and started my trek to work. It was so cold that I never even looked up to greet the tower guards as I usually did. They never came out of the guard tower either. I reached the entrance of the facility at the same time as the Boss was entering.

"Good morning Doctor." I bid him good morning, also. "Did you get a chance to see the paper this morning?" I hadn't, the usual copy of the "Journal" was not in the staff dining room, and I asked what had I missed? "Front page news, Henry, Queen Victoria has passed away. She was 81 years old and passed on Tuesday, New Year's Day. The article said that she reigned for 63 years." It was kind of a shock to me. Victoria had been Queen all my life. "The paper said that plans were being made to coronate Edward king." A quick jog of the mind and my old history lessons that would be Edward the VII. "Sorry for the loss of your Queen, Henry." I thanked the Boss for his sympathy, but I reminded the Warden I was an American now. "Just the same, old man, she was a part of the heart of your former country all your life. Also, I kind of liked the old girl." I agreed that she was a good Monarch and the people loved her.

The Warden went up the iron stair case to his office and I went to the kitchen for my weekly inspection, before heading to the infirmary to start sick call.

Many of the inmate complaints were minor aches and pains or winter colds etc. With the invention of aspirin, my treatment of minor problems such as these, gave much relief to my patients. It gave the prisoners the impression that I was a miracle worker taking away their discomfort. This new medicine seemed to relieve pain and also reduced fever. Truly it was an amazing new product.

Much of the State's industry surrounded around the textile industry. There was a large influx of immigrants coming into Rhode Island from Europe, mostly from Ireland and Italy. Many of the Irish and Italians worked in textile factories along the rivers in the State. The owners of the factories became very influential politically and lobbied against prison made goods being sold on the open market. Much of the prison's income came from the sales of shirts made by prisoner labor, along with other items manufactured by their work. There is a move by the State to prohibit the sale of prison goods to the public. The Warden has been successful in maintaining the status quo so far. We have discussed, at the Boss's staff meetings, of ways to maintain production and alternatives to some of the goods being sold.

At one of our meetings the Warden came up with an idea to reach out to some of the business owners with a proposal that could help with the reformatory project. He suggested that they may be open to using prisoners in a training program for young prisoners to learn a trade that they could use in their businesses. It would almost be like an apprenticeship program and the prisoner would work for that business when they were released. Many changes were on the horizon.

There were other States that were making progress in the treatment of the poor and mentally ill. In the Southern New England area I was becoming known as a reformer here in Rhode Island. I began accompanying Dr. Keene and other prominent people to meetings in Massachusetts and Connecticut. I found myself becoming consumed with social issues.

I was called to report to the Warden's office before I left for the day. After finishing my duties, I climbed the iron staircase to the Boss's office. It was a familiar walk lately. I knocked on the large oak door. After a few seconds delay, I heard the Warden beckon me in. I entered to find him seated at his desk in his jacket and tie. A signal that this was not a social call. "Thank you doctor for stopping in. Please take a seat." I sat at the side of his desk.

"Doctor, I know that you have been busy with promoting mental health and prison reform. Your activities have also not gone unnoticed down town. I have been getting some inquiries about you from some "friends" in the legislature. They are raising some concerns that you may be slacking on your duties here at the prison. I have assured them that you have not and that actually your time here as our doctor has been very fruitful and actually you have been a God send to not only the prisoners but to staff. "I did remind them of you work during the typhoid outbreak as an example." I thanked him for his support.

"I don't understand what the problem is. My activities have all been done openly. I have not been critical of our State nor anyone in State service. Dr. Keene has been aware of everything and has accompanied me whenever I have been asked to speak on issues of treatment of those on the fringes of our society." The General stood and walked to the hooks on the office wall and removed his jacket hanging it on one.

"Henry, you know that part of my job is not only running the jail and prison. There are other things of a political nature that is a crucial part of being the Warden. This is an election year. That means that all the cockroaches come out and are looking for causes to chew on or political foes to crawl over. Of late I have been a target of some old political enemies. They say I have been here to long and am getting too old to do the job, and some evil talk involving prison funds, with my nephew Frank and records and things. Some are trying to use you to get at me. It appears that Garvin is running for Governor. He would be the first Democrat elected Governor in Rhode Island in many years. If elected he will be looking to appoint as many of his supporters to State positions as he can, it is looking like that just may happen."

I began to see just how shrewd the Boss was. My

eyes were opened on how Nelson was able to lead the prison for so many years. It was more than his reputation as a war hero and a good administrator. He knew people. He could read people and almost see into their heart and soul. Now I understand why he has given me the lead on many of the changes made at the prison. He really needs to maintain his reputation politically as well as with the staff and inmates.

"I will tell my "Friends" that I had a talk with you on your activities and am satisfied that there is nothing to be concerned about." I thanked him again for his support. "Just remember, Henry that all those people that are shaking your hand and patting you on your back are not your friends and supporters. They will turn on you, and bury their dagger in your back to the hilt if you are not careful. Doctor Keene is a good man and is highly supportive of you. However there are several members of the Board of Charity and Corrections that feel threatened with changes that you and Keene have been talking about. They don't want to see changes, and profit from the status quo. These guys have friends downtown that also enjoy things the way they are." I found myself nodding my head, as my eyes were opened on to what the Boss was saying.

"I understand, Warden. Thank you for the information and the insight into the situation going on. Maybe I should cut back on speaking out on issues of prison and mental health reform."

"No, no, Henry. You keep up the good thing you

are doing. It is important things you are doing. There are many that agree with the need to change the treatment of patients in State care. Just remember our conversation and also that change comes slowly and sometimes with great pain. I think we will be alright even if Garvin gets elected. The Republicans will still hold power in the Legislature and that's who controls the purse strings." Our conversation was more than a warning to be careful in my activities and whom I shared my ideas with, I realized that I was being schooled just in case something were to take place and the Boss were to be replaced.

"Thank you, again, for your support. I understand that this conversation is just between us, and I will keep my eyes and ears open and keep you informed if I get wind of anything that may be coming down. Sometimes people talk around me while not giving a thought that I may hear what they are saying. Oh, and you don't have to remind me what happens or what is said in prison stays in prison." We both broke into laughter. We shook hands and I left from my quarters at the residence hall.

The whole year of 1902 was hectic. The population of the prison and jail was on the increase again. Overcrowding has always been an issue since I began my career as the prison physician. The Boss spent a lot of time in Providence cementing support for the prison operations. I have noticed that it is taking its toll on him. He is beginning to look older.

The warden left word with Frank to have me come to his office. He told me that they had been working on a report to the Board of Charities and Corrections. The new Chairman of the Board, George Smith, wanted the Warden to make his annual report in person before the Board. The annual report was usually a written report. This time he was to submit a written report to them and appear in person in the event they had any "questions". I headed up stairs to see the Boss.

I knocked and entered at same time he had call me to come in. "Henry, thank you for stopping in." I told him Frank had told me you wanted to see me. "I would like you along with Frank to accompany me to meet with the Board. I want to be prepared for any questions they may have. I can't just depend on my memory for details. So I want Frank to back me up on facts and figures and, if you would, be there in case there are questions on medical issues or conditions." I told the Boss that I would be happy to attend with him.

"Good, thanks Henry. You may want to jot down some notes on numbers of prisoners treated any deaths and causes. Also maybe an opportunity to talk again about the crowding issue from a medical point of view." I assured him I would be ready to speak on all medical problems and to maybe brag a little on our successes. He did crack a smile. "Good, the three of us will ride up together next Monday. We are scheduled to appear at 1 o'clock." I bid the Boss good bye and headed to my office in the infirmary to gather some facts and figures to take to my apartment and review.

We arrived about fifteen minutes early and could hear muffled conversations coming from the Boardroom. The door opened and we were called in. The Board of Directors were seated with Chairman Smith in the center.

"Good afternoon gentlemen. Thank you for attending the meeting of the Board of Charities and Corrections. Being the new Chairman of the Board I wanted to meet all of the units' management heads in person this year not just read the annual reports. It is nice to finally meet you, Warden Viall. You have gained quite a reputation as Warden of our facility. Please introduce the gentlemen accompanying you today."

While we stood at the table in front of the Board. The General walked forward to about three feet in front of the Director. Standing over him he began. "Thank you for the opportunity to address the Board in person." Half turning towards us he introduced Frank as the Chief Clerk of the prison and myself as the Prison Physician. The General was at the top of his game. He took full command of the room. By the expression on his face, the Chairman was definitely intimidated and questioning his decision of having the Warden make an in person report. I observed several of the long time Board Members had slight smiles on their faces.

"Please take a seat, Warden." The Boss turned and slowly walked to the table giving Frank and me a little wink. "Warden could you please give myself and the

Board an overview of the Jail and Prison operation?" That was the opening of the door.

"Mr. Chairman, Our system is upon the congregate plan. We have for the past forty years let the labor to outside parties, who contract for a term of years. During that time the prisoners have been constantly employed. We work our men in the manufacture of boots and shoes, also shirts, mops and brooms advertising for bids, it provides that the instructors are also trainers. I prefer our system to the State-account or piece-price plan. With our system there is less friction with outside business............Our number of prisoners is 190.....The County jail is under the same management, with a population of 300. The same officers and provisions are provided for both institutions.....No officer is permitted to strike or injure an inmate unless in self-defense. Various privileges are accorded to those in the first grade, such as frequent visits of friends, a larger cell, more frequent correspondence, limited use of tobacco, etc........Officers are employed and take the lower grade of pay." The Chairman interrupted and asked about political appointments of staff. "No political influence is brought to bear, and for nearly thirty years I have never been influenced by politicians." The Warden continued. "We have a resident chaplain, who with the Catholic clergy, devotes the forenoon on the Sabbath to religious worship, with good results. A good library is prized very highly, all principal magazines are added monthly. We have 1,700 volumes. We recently added evening school in October....

Frank began to slide papers in front of the Warden. "The number of recidivists is fully 30 per cent. Four years ago our legislature passed a habitual-criminal act, which gives a sentence of twenty-five years for the third offense of a penal character. This it is hoped, will deter the repeaters of crime in this State." The Boss turned to me and asked that I speak regarding Medical Services, and disease control at the facility.

"Mr. Chairman, being the Prison Physician is challenging. With men being committed with a variety of existing physical conditions, it is important to ensure that disease is not being introduced into the prison from outside. Each new prisoner is held in quarantine until being seen by the physician before being place into the general population.....in recent years we have had two major out breaks of disease, typhoid and cholera both were eradicated and their causes discovered and corrected.......The main existing problem is adequate housing for the population. The temporary wooden housing did help for a short time however it appears that this temporary fix is becoming permanent.....the Warden has assured me that the Board is aware and sympathetic to the situation and is awaiting approval of the legislature for funding to correct the housing issue. The Chairman interrupted my presentation and pitch for reform, and thanked me for my thorough presentation on the medical issues. I noticed the Boss smiling at me.

Our appearance before the Board of Charity and Corrections lasted just over two hours. We had answers for all issues raised. Even when the Chairman brought up the fact that Frank and the Warden were related. The Warden's answer brought laughter from the whole Board even its Chairman. "This is a small State, Mr. Chairman, and if we disqualified relatives from State employment because of who they know or are related to, we would have to seek workers from other states."

November 11th, election day. The Boss made sure that the whole staff had the opportunity to vote. He ordered the prisoners locked down and went on a Sunday schedule. Every staff member was given, if they wished, a ride to the polls. They all wished. November 11, 1902 was my first opportunity to vote in my adopted country. I thought my back was going to break with the Boss patting me on the back. His hands and arms had lost none of their strength from his days working in the foundry.

The election for Governor was a loss for the Republicans. Lucius Garvin was elected Rhode Island's new Governor. The Republicans maintained the House and Senate. In reality the strongest political position in the State was the Speaker of the House. However the Governor made many of the appointments to key positions including the Warden of the Jail and Prison. He is advised by the Board of Charity and Corrections. Chairman Smith is no fan of the Warden's. Most of the Board Members are behind the Boss. He has made them look good for many years and are loyal to him. I marvel as I have been schooled by the Boss on the political intrigue in Rhode Island, of which the Warden is a Master.

The inauguration of the new Governor was held at the old State House at 150 Benefit Street. The Warden was at the ceremony, the "Good Soldier" that he is.

Following the inauguration the Boss came back to work. I found him, Frank Viall and Ed Slocum in Ed's office talking. I knock and went in. The atmosphere was lite and happier than I had expected.

"Good afternoon gentlemen." They all greeted me warmly. "Well, Sir how did the inauguration go?" I asked, almost holding my breath.

"The biggest group of assholes I've ever seen since my days in the army shower room." I almost past out from laughter. "I think that I will be remaining as Warden. I spoke with Garvin after the ceremony and he asked me to stay on, for a while at least. He spoke about needing a connection that has friends in the Legislature. His political people had mentioned to him that I could be that person. We will see how it goes."

Winter was difficult. One of the snowiest in many years. The walk to work was difficult. Charlie made sure that he cut me a path through the snow from the Residence hall down the hill to the prison. Some of the real bad days he showed up with the sleigh to give me a ride to work. The Warden has had a little difficulty breathing for the past few years a combination of asthma, his weight and age. The damp cold weather did not help.

I pictured our meetings in my mind and drifted back to our first meeting just before I was hired. It was quite......................... BANG! BANG! BANG!!!

CHAPTER 14
THEY JUST FADE AWAY

I woke with a start! The sound of someone pounding on my door. The room was dark and my eyes blurred from sleep, and my mind confused from my dreams. I made my way to the door. "Who is it?" I called. The voice from the other side.

"Doctor, it's Jim Wardle, guard at the prison. I've been sent to fetch you. It's the Warden. You need to come quick, we can't wake him. He sounds just terrible." I opened the door. There was a uniformed guard, his size filled my doorway.

"Come in man, come in. Calm yourself man and, tell me again, what has happened?"

"The night guard, assigned to watch over the Boss, err, the Warden, sir, he reported to the Captain that the Warden is in great difficulty in his trying to breathe. He be gasping for each breath. The lad was not able to wake him. The Captain has sent me to fetch you, and bring you to him, with haste! "

As I readied myself to leave, I grabbed my coat and medical bag. "What time is it man? Has The Warden's housekeeper come to the house yet?"

"No sir. She has not arrive yet. It is early for her. It is now only a quarter past five, sir. I am to go fetch her, after coming for you. Please hurry doctor! I will go now for Mrs. Flynn and raise a neighbor to sit with the children until school."

I left my residence into a cool Friday, May 1st morning. The sun had not risen, the sky was a greenish blue signaling the sun's appearance in the eastern sky. I could see the black silhouette of the prison against the lighting sky. I rushed towards its massive stone walls, praying that I am not too late to assist my old colleague now friend. There was light coming from the windows of the gray stone, Warden's residence. Standing in the doorway was a guard armed with a rifle to insure no one entered except those summonsed to help the General. Word had spread of the Warden's condition and it was time for the day shift to report for duty. The Captain had wisely assigned a man to keep the guards, reporting and leaving the prison, from coming to check on their boss. The Warden was well liked and respected among the staff. And the concern for him would outweigh their good sense, putting them in the way.

"Good morning, Sir. Go right up, Sir. Captain McCauley is with him in the bedroom. I am to keep all the other men away from disturbing you and the good Warden."

"Thank you man, be true to your post and orders. Please send Mrs. Flynn up stairs when she arrives. I will be needing her assistance with the General." When Deputy Warden Slocum arrives, please tell him I will keep him informed on the Warden's condition. I am sure he will be busy with prison business today." Ed Slocum, was a capable man. He is dedicated to the General. His uncle served with the Warden in the war before being killed at the battle of Bull Run in '61". I learned early on, that the General was a man who surrounded himself with men he felt he could trust, men that he knew well, or had trained himself. The Warden knew politics well and how a small slip of the tongue or misinformation can ruin a reputation or a career. One of his favorite expressions was, "What happens in prison stays in prison."

I topped the stairs, knocked on the bedroom door. "Come in, come in. Oh doctor, thank God you're here. The General is not responding to me. I have been trying to rouse him. He is having great difficulty breathing and I believe he may have a fever." The Captain stepped away from the bed side giving me access to his Boss.

I laid my hand on the large man's forehead. It was clammy and warm. I removed my stethoscope from my bag, and listened to my broad chested friend's heart. His heart beat was weak. I threw the blanket off that was covering his body to see his feet and ankles. Both feet and ankles were severely swollen. I covered him back up with just the sheet. "Captain, can you give me a hand with the Warden? I need to sit him up to listen to his lungs." The Captain went to the other side of the bed and together we lifted the large man forward. As the Captain held him in place, I placed the stethoscope to his back. His breathing is labored, and shallow and much worse than yesterday. We laid him back down. The Captain looked over to me from across the bed, with tears in his eyes.

"Doctor, will you be able to help him? Is there anything I can do to help? The General is much more than my employer. My own mother was good friends with Mary, God Bless Her Sainted Soul. It was because of her that I am in his employ, and have charge over the prison at night. When I was lad the General hired me on as a policeman, trained me, and brought me with him when he was named Warden. The man has been like my own father, he has. I do love the man, and wouldn't want to lose him."

"I don't want to give you false hope, William. He is a very sick man. His kidneys seem to have shut down and his heart and lungs are involved. I assure you, I will do all I can for him and make him as comfortable as I can." We were interrupted by Maureen rushing into the room.

"Oh Lord, Doctor is the General dead!"

"No, but he is much worse than when I saw him

yesterday. He is not conscious, his heart is not well and his lungs are involved." I turned to the Captain. "Captain, thank you for your help and attention to the boss. You should go home and get your sleep. You are well past your shift and you will be needed again to-night. I will keep the Deputy informed on the Wardens condition and I am sure he will keep the men updated."

"If you are sure there is nothing I can do, I will leave and be out of your way. I will be stopping at the church on the way home, lighting a candle and leav-ing a prayer for him." Tipping his uniform cap, "Mrs. Flynn, thank you for coming so quickly. I hope my man did not frighten you at your door so early." Maureen smiled back at the Captain.

"No Captain. I am pleased to be here, and be help-ing' the fine doctor with the General."

"Maureen, could you please go and fetch a basin of water and some cloths and towels. We need to try to bring his fever down. Oh, and a cup of tea will be of help also." The housekeeper gave me a strange look. I smiled at her. "The tea would be for me, dear." She returned the smile and left the room.

Alone with him I took his hand, "Warden." There was no response. "Nelson, Nelson it's Henry, Henry Jones, can you hear me man?" His large hand closed slowly and weakly around mine. My mind flashed an image of our first meeting and how his large hand gripped mine, firm and strong, a hand that was no stranger to hard labor.

"Good, I am here for you. I will do all I can, but you are very sick. You need to hang on and stay with us. Maureen, and I will try to get your fever down. That should make you more alert. We need you to help fight this fever off, and stay with us."

Just then the housekeeper came back into the bedroom. "I have your tea and a few biscuits for you, doctor. I know that you had no time for a breakfast this morning. I will put the water and cloths over here." She placed the tea on the small table near the chair where I was seated, and the basin of water on the table near the window.

"Thank you. The biscuits was very thoughtful of you. I have not eaten since dinner last evening. They look delightful." I ate one with a sip of my tea, and took another from the plate, as she asked.

"Is there any change, doctor? He does look and sound terrible." I raised my finger to my lips, shook my head and mouthed the words that he could hear us. "Oh good Lord." She responded. "What will you be needing me to do, doctor?"

"Give me a hand removing the General's nightshirt." Maureen unbuttoned the two buttons at the neck and I reached down under the sheet grasping the hem and pulled up around his body to his chest. The Housekeeper took one side and me the other and pulled it up and over his head. "Aar, there we go." The garment was soaked with sweat. Maureen rolled it up and threw it on to the chair at the foot of the bed.

"Now if you would be so kind to wet one of the towels, ring it out, and put it over his chest. Fine that's it, now if you could sit with him and keep a cool cloth to his forehead and change it as need when it gets warm. This will draw the heat out from the fever. Every little while if you could change the towel to a cool one would be good also. I will be back shortly. I am going to report to the Deputy on the General's condition, and I have to send word to the Superintendent so he can inform the Board of Charities of the Warden's condition. I will return within the hour."

I went down the stairs and out the front door. A guard was still on post. "Good morning doctor, how is the General doing?"

"Good morning. He is holding on. But he is very sick. I will be back shortly. I have to speak to your Deputy." I rounded the corner of the residence and entered the prison, and proceeded to the office of the Deputy Warden. I knocked and was summoned in. Ed Slocum was seated at his desk reading daily reports. "Good morning Deputy."

"Is it? The Deputy asked. "How is the boss doing? Will he be all right?" Captain McCauley gave me a full report on the events of the night. I've been waiting to hear an update."

"The Captain is a fine man, and took charge of the situation. You should rest well with him in charge during the night. As you know I was alerted to the Warden's condition early this morning. I rushed right over and found him in very grave danger. His lungs and heart are fully involved and he was unconscious. I had sent for Mrs. Flynn and the good Captain helped me move him so I could examine him further. When Mrs. Flynn arrived we have been working to try to lower his temperature. She is with him now. He is able to hear us and indicated so even though he is not able to speak at this time." The Deputy stood and turned towards the window overlooking the prison yard. Without turning around he asked.

"Doctor, will he make it.? He has been a good friend to my whole family. Writing to the family after John was killed in the war. The whole family is very fond of the General. And, for myself, I have never known a better man than himself."

"The next few hours will tell. I am hopeful, but not confident he will pull out of this one. He is up in years and has had a tough life. But he is strong willed, and a tough man. Really Ed it is up to him. I will do all I can for him. I need to write a report to the Superintendent. May I used your desk for a little while?"

"Of course doctor. I have to walk the prison and check on things. Am I able to talk of the boss's condition to the lads? They are all concerned for him and are worried."

"Yes, of course. Assure them that I am doing my very best for him and they would do well the send a little prayer up for him. I will be asking the good Reverend Nutting to put in a good word for the General with the Man up Stairs." The Deputy took his leave, and I started my written report to the Superintendent and copy to the State Board.

When I finished I went to see Frank Viall. Frank is the Clerk for the prison. I want to let him know how Nelson is doing, so he can keep the family updated. The Warden has long been the patriarch of the Viall family and I am sure Frank has already got the word out to the clan that he is in bad shape. I entered the Clerk's Office. Frank stood and reached across the desk to welcome me.

"How is he doing, doctor? Thank you for stopping in to see me. I know you are busy with Nelson."

"Frank it's not going well. The General is very sick. His lungs and heart are congested, and his kidneys have shut down. Most men don't come back from being this ill. I will do all I can for him but, to tell you the truth, I fear that he is dying. You may want to let the family know that it is a very good possibility he won't make it."

"Thank you for coming so quickly. I spoke to Captain McCauley before he left for home this morning. He told me about how he looked before he left for home. He said it didn't look good."

"Frank, could you see that this report gets over to the Superintendent and ask that he inform the Board Chairman about the Warden?" As I handed the letter to the Clerk, the guard who was at the front door of the residence busted into the Clerk's Office.

"Doctor! Mrs. Flynn sent me to get you, it's the Warden Sir. He has taken a bad turn and she needs you to come now."

I ran out of the office, Frank and the guard were on my heels. The guard resumed his post at the entrance to the house. Frank passed me on the stairs and we both entered the bedroom together. Maureen was seated holding the Warden's hand. She turned towards us. "Oh, doctor he's been speaking. He's been thinking that I'm Mary, Bless her Soul. He told me he was cold so I removed the towel from him and put a blanket over him. His fever seems to be down, but his breathing is awful. He stopped breathing and I thought he was dead. Then he gasped back to life. Then he stops again and gasps back again. Oh doctor, the poor man is suffering so."

I grabbed my stethoscope from my bag. "Frank give me a hand will you. Help me sit him up so I can listen to his lungs." Together we sat him up so I could reach his back. I shook my head to Frank. We laid him back down and I put the stethoscope to his chest. He gave out another gasp for air. His heart beats were few and far between. Again I shook my head to the on lookers. Both Maureen and Frank had tears in their eyes.

"I did everything you told me, Doctor, just as you said."

I assured Maureen that she did a fine job and that she did all she could. I then asked if she could go and make me a small lunch as it was well past time for lunch. I told her she should have a bit herself. She nodded in agreement, and left Frank and I alone with the General. Frank took Maureen's place in the chair next to the bed and took the General's hand. His breathing was shallow and intermittent. After about ten minutes the General took another gasping breath, and stopped breathing. Frank turned looking at me. I took my stethoscope and listened again closely to his chest. I listened for about five minutes. Nothing. I shook my head to Frank. "He's gone, Frank."

A tear rolled down the cheek of the Clerk. I heard Maureen top the stairs. I went to the bedroom door and took the tray that was holding a sandwich a cup of coffee and piece of pie. "He has passed Maureen. He's with Mary, his beloved wife and their children." She slowly walked to the bed, resting her right hand on Frank's shoulder and the other on the General's hand. Tears flowed down her face.

Nelson Viall, Veteran of two wars, a General, State Representative, Chief of Police, and Prison Warden of 36 years, passed away in his bed with relative and friends about him. Man has only one death it should not be wasted, the Boss didn't waste his. He died his way as the Boss.

My work was not done. I took my watch from my vest pocket. It was Twelve minutes past two in the afternoon, Friday May 3rd in year of our Lord 1903. Cause of Death, Congestive Heart and Acute Renal Failure. Attending Physician, Henry A. Jones........

CHAPTER 15

TAPS

Howard – Nelson Viall, 75 Passed away at his residence on Friday May 3, 1903. A prominent figure in the State of Rhode Island. Born in Plainfield Connecticut. A Veteran of the war with Mexico, serving as a Sargent with Co. A 9th Infantry, US Volunteers, Commanded by Col. Ambrose. And in the Great War between the States, serving with the 1st RI Militia, 2nd RI Infantry, under his old commander Col. Burnside. He later commanded the 14th RI Heavy Artillery (Colored Regiment). He rose through the ranks to Brigadier General, participating in several major battles, to include, 1st Battle of Bull Run; and Fredericksburg. At Mechanicsville, VA., he was wounded in the hip at Seven Pines.

Following the war, he served a term in the State Legislature and was appointed Chief of Police in Providence. In 1867 was appointed Warden of the Providence County Jail and State Prison, opening the new prison in Howard, RI in 1878, where he has served until his death.

Warden Viall was the husband of the late Mary Viall, father of the late Willard, Arthur, Mary and Ellen Viall. He will lie in state at his residence at the State Prison. His funeral will take place at Lakeside-Carpenter Cemetery, E. Providence on Tuesday May 7th at 10:00am with full Military Honors. (Providence Journal, May 4, 1903)

I checked my watch, 9:40am, a large crowd was

still gathering at Lakeside Cemetery. The who's who of the State were gathering. The General was well known and well respected by everyone. The newly elected Governor Garvin was speaking with a group of the members of the Board of Corrections and Charities, he was shaking hands with George Smith the Chairman. I'm sure discussing future plans for the prison administration. What was most impressive, to me, were the large number of regular citizens of the state that were present. Not to my surprise was Old Charlie dressed in his "Sunday Go To Meeting" clothes. There were old gentlemen, some in faded uniform. Standing separated from the large group was approximately a dozen Negro gentlemen. They were standing at military parade rest, one was in his faded uniform and another had a guide arm indicating the 14th Artillery. Everyone turned in unison as we heard the sound of horses' hooves on the cobblestone road of the cemetery. The caisson bearing the body of General Viall draped in the United States Flag, flanked by eight soldiers. Leading the precession were about twenty supervisors and guards from the prison. Lastly Reverend Nutting followed with the General's family.

The procession stopped near the open grave that was waiting to receive its eternal occupant. The family monument marking the family's grave site was a tall granite pillar topped with an urn the base was inscribe with the names of Nelson's wife and children. The military bearers lifted the coffin from the caisson.

With military precision carried their fallen Conrad to a stand aside the grave. Coming forward the Reverend Nutting, Prison Chaplin, lead the mourners in prayer and shared a few words of memories he had accumulated about the Warden. When finished the Major in charge of the Military Honor Guard, called detail to "Attention!"

I looked around at the gathered crowd. The Military, Prison Guards, and uniformed Police present snapped to attention. I looked over at the aged members of the 14th. All stood as straight as pokers. "Ready, FIRE!" as the rifle salute echoed across the cemetery, a short distance away a cannon blast, answered the rifle fire, its retort shaking the soft ground we were standing on. A military bugler and drummer stepped forward of the riflemen. "HAND SALUTE!" the Major called out, the drummer began a muted drum roll, as the bugler lifted the instrument to his lips. The bugle call, TAPS echoed mournfully across the cemetery grounds.

"REST IN PEACE OLD FRIEND"

AFTERWARD

Many changes came to the Institutions at Howard. The prison built in 1878 is still in use. It took until 1924 for an addition of 198 cells to be added to the south wing, and the wooden "temporary" structure to be torn down. The Reformatory idea caught on and a Men's Reformatory was constructed east of the State Prison in 1932, segregating the younger men from those housed in the prison. The facility consisted of four dormitories one of which had a small cellblock to house disciplinary problems. The Rhode Island State Prison grew over the years. In 1956 the small county jails in Newport and Kent Counties closed. Staff and inmates were transferred to the Providence County jail at the Prison facility. And in 1972 the Adult Correctional Institutions were created, encompassing the jails, reformatory and the prison.

Reformers like Doctors Henry Jones, George Keene,

and William McCaw laid the foundation for changes to the State Hospital and newly formed Institute for Mental Health. Followed by other prominent doctors such as Dr. Arthur Harrington who as the new Superintendent broke down the policy of isolation and the public were instructed as to the great needs of the institutions for the mental patients.

In 1976 the Legislature created the Rhode Island Department of Corrections, naming Anthony P. Travisono as its first Department Director. The Department originally encompassing the Boy's and Girl's School, the State's Jail, Men's and the Women's Reformatory (Medium/Minimum Security). Also included were the Probation and Parole sections, and the Providence County Sherif's Committing Squad. The Poor Farm had long ago been closed. The Prison Farm slowly closed. The last of the dairy herd was sold by late 1969. Only a small "Garden" operation continued into the 1980's. By 1978 the Boy's and Girl's Training School were move under the Department of Youth, Children and Families.

In the 1980's new prison facilities were being built. Due to Federal Law Suits, the Intake Service Center was built to house inmates that were awaiting trial and those newly sentenced. The area used for the jail became part of Maximum Security (the old prison/jail facility). At the same time, due to a number of escapes and the murder of a Correctional Officer, a High Security Center was built. Removing the most dangerous and aggressive inmates from the old prison building.

Women inmates that were being housed in Massachusetts, because of the small numbers, were returned to the State and housed in a facility that had been used as part of the Boy's Training school. Then moved again to a building that was part of the Mental Health Hospital and renovated for a Women's Prison.

In early 1992 a New Medium Security Facility was built and occupied. The Reformatory building continued to be used as a low Medium Security Facility.

The mental health system in the State changed drastically in the late 60's and 70's. The State's policy changed to community treatment and housing of patients. Many of the old Mental Health buildings were put to other uses. To include Corrections Training Facility, Minimum and Work Release Facilities of the Corrections Department.

Following the death of Warden Viall, Hunter White took over as Acting Warden lasting one month. He was replaced by Warden Andrew Willcox whose term lasted only seven months. Over the years a number of noteworthy men served as Warden at the prison. The 1950's Warden Gore, in the 1960's a retired FBI Agent Harold V. Langlois became Warden. He was the last to live in the Warden's Residence. The Warden's house became office space. Warden Langlois departure in 1969, brought about a number of temporary or Acting Wardens. This period was a time of great turmoil. There were a number of inmate law suits and court rulings that brought about many operational changes. Maximum Security (the old State Prison) became a very violent place. The violent conditions, and Union unrest, continued. Following the stabling and death of a Correctional Officer in the 1980's, came the appointment of an experienced prison administrator, John J. Moran. He brought organization and discipline, he was well respected by the staff and was popular with the political powers, being a stabilizing figure within the Department. As the Department expanded, it became clear that one man could not oversee all the facilities and operations. Slowly additional Wardens were added. The last Warden to serve alone was Donald O. Ellerthorpe, a retired Army Colonel whom had been the commandant at Fort Leavenworth's Military Prison. Some of the notable past Wardens of the Maximum Security Facility were James Mullen, retired State Police Detective, Walter Whitman, James Weeden both of whom came up through the ranks at the Department. Warden Nelson Viall still hold the record for the longest serving Warden of the Rhode Island State Prison.

Currently there are a number of Wardens serving at various facilities of the Rhode Island Department of Correction. One oversees Maximum and High Security, another for Medium Security, one for Minimum and Work Release, and another for the Women's Facility. Also there is a Warden overseeing the Intake Service Center which serves as the States Jail within the State's unified style of operation.

BIBLIOGRAPHY

The Dark Days of Social Welfare at the State Institutions 1943, Printed by E.L. Freeman

Dr. Henry A. Jones

R.I. Board of Charities and Corrections Reports 1893 thru 1903.

State Archives,

RI, Secretary of State

Nelson Viall Papers

RI Historical Society, Manuscript Division

Statewide Historical Preservation Report P-C-1 For Cranston, RI 1970

RI Historical Preservation Commission

The National & Rhode Island: Military Order Of the Loyal Legion of the U.S., Mollus War Papers

Transcribed by Gregg A. Mierka

The RI GAR 1st RI Volunteer Infantry/First Infantry RIM Civil War History

GAR Civil War Museum Library and Research Ctr.

"Happy 150th Providence Police"

The Providence Journal August 12, 2014

RI Adjutant General's Report on Units of the Civil War, 1893

Elisha Dyer, Jr.

BIBLIOGRAPHY

Nashua City Station Railroad History Picture

Nashuacitystation.org